EPIC

HISTORIC ADVENTURES

A Great Escape

Felice Arena is one of Australia's best-loved
children's writers. He is the author and creator of
many popular and award-winning children's books
for all ages, including the acclaimed
The Boy and the Spy and *A Great Escape*.

This book is dedicated to my long-time editor and friend Michelle Madden.

First American Edition 2023
Kane Miller, A Division of EDC Publishing

Cover images: Silhouette of woman on high wall © Kamil Vojnar/Trevillion Images; 1946's boy walking on brick wall © Mark Owen/Trevillion Images; Sky, Bright Blue,Orange And Yellow Colors Sunset by Grisha Bruev; and Abstract chaotic lines pattern by Yes - Royalty Free/Shutterstock.com

For information contact:
Kane Miller, A Division of EDC Publishing
5402 S 122nd E Ave
Tulsa, OK 74146
www.kanemiller.com

Library of Congress Control Number: 2022934496

Printed and bound in the United States of America
1 2022

ISBN: 978-1-68464-539-8

A Great Escape

Felice Arena

Kane Miller
A DIVISION OF EDC PUBLISHING

Verräter
TRAITOR

Peter is riding as fast as he can. He stands up out of his seat and crunches down on the pedals. He steers his bike toward a long plank of wood propped up on a small stack of bricks. It's the perfect launching ramp.

He hollers as he makes contact with the plank and rides up the ramp at top speed.

"YAAAAA!" Peter yanks the handlebars up toward his chest to get some lift. He keeps pedaling, then he's airborne! Flying!

The wheels hit the cobblestones with a bouncy thud. Peter almost loses his balance as he kicks back on his right pedal and slams the brakes. The bike skids, the back tire fishtails from side to side, and Peter drops his left foot and drags it on the ground. He stops and looks back at the ramp set up in the middle of his street.

"Yes!" he hisses, as his friends Max and Hubert run up to him.

Hubert takes a piece of chalk from his pocket and scratches a line across the cobblestones. "The back wheel hit the ground right here," he says excitedly. "But Max still holds the record. Just. See!"

The boys look down, and Peter sees that Max's chalk line is a few centimeters ahead of his own mark.

Peter winces. "I'll go again."

"Give it up, Peter," says Max. "You'll never beat me."

But Peter is already riding back to take another jump.

"Peter!" It's his mother's voice from a window of his apartment. Peter looks up at her. They live in one of the older buildings, one of only a few in the street that survived the bombs and bullets of the war. Its dark-gray brick and large crisscross windows make it stand out from all the others around it. Most of the street is lined with dull-looking concrete slab apartment buildings.

"Time to come in. We're leaving soon. I won't tell

you again," she shouts, before closing the shutters.

Peter ignores her. He stares back toward the ramp, determined to beat Max's record. But before he takes off, a car turns onto the street.

Hubert and Max run to grab the makeshift ramp and drag it to the curb.

The car rolls by slowly, avoiding the piles of bricks.

Stefan Fischer, who lives in Peter's building, is in the back seat. He waves at them.

"Bye, Peter!" he shouts out from the back window. "Bye, Max! Hubert! Perhaps we'll see you over there."

Peter waves, and watches Stefan and his family drive away.

"That's the tenth boy from our school who has moved to the West just in the last week," says Hubert. "Anyone with family to stay with over there is leaving. Are you moving too, Peter?"

Peter shrugs. "I don't know. My dad works there, so I guess we could. They say over in the West you're free. You can earn more money and buy whatever you want –" But that's all Peter manages to say before Max interrupts him.

"They're all deserters," he snaps. "Stefan is just another *Verräter*, a traitor – that's what my father says. They're all capitalist traitors. They'll regret it."

"That's not what my brother Ralf says," Hubert

exclaims. "He says that after the war this city should have been divided up between the Americans, the English and the French. Nothing should have gone to the Soviet Union. He said we've drawn the short straw – the Soviets hate us Germans."

"Your brother is wrong," Max snaps. "How can he say that? Everyone is equal here. Your brother is the biggest *Verräter* of them all!"

"You take that back!" Hubert cries.

"Make me," says Max.

Peter shakes his head as his friends break out into a familiar argument.

It's all that anyone is talking about these days – the thousands of people moving from East Berlin over to the western parts of the city.

Max steps up to Hubert and shoves him. Hubert shoves Max back. Their biting words have turned into a scuffle.

Peter throws down the bike and steps in between his friends – trying his best to separate them.

"Stop fighting, boys. For goodness' sake, Peter!" His mother has now made her way downstairs and is stepping out onto the street. She's holding Peter's little sister Margrit's hand. "*Komm, sofort!* Come, immediately!"

Margrit nods, her mop of blond messy curls falling

over her rosy cheeks.

"Hang on, Mutti," Peter yells, as Max manages to snatch Hubert's glasses off him. "Just give me a minute."

"Too late!" she calls. "You'll have to stay home with Opa and Oma. We'll be back tomorrow night."

Peter's mother turns and Margrit waves to him, before they disappear back inside the apartment building.

"Give the glasses back to him," Peter says, turning to Max. "Stop being a *Dummkopf*."

"I can't see without them," complains Hubert.

Max steps back a few steps. "If you want them, Hubert, you can come and get them." Then he turns and bolts down the footpath.

Peter swings into action. He runs back to the bike and gives chase. He pedals as fast as he can. Max is on foot, but he has a good head start. He turns onto the next street, and runs onto a narrow footbridge arching over a stormwater drain.

Peter makes a swift decision to cut Max off. The road section is shorter than the footbridge, so he knows he can get ahead of Max. He will have to jump the drain to cut him off, but he's pretty sure he can do it.

He avoids the footbridge and continues to ride

on the street. The boys race each other on either side of the drain. Peter gets out in front of Max. The drain narrows slightly and Peter knows this is the moment. He takes a sharp turn.

Here goes! he thinks.

Peter stands up out of his seat, pulls up on the handlebars and . . . soars clear over the ditch. He lands and skids to a stop directly in front of Max, who is caught off guard. The bike drops. Peter grabs hold of Max and they wrestle each other, first standing, and then rolling around on the ground.

Peter overpowers Max. He sits on his chest, pinning him down, and snatches Hubert's glasses out of his pocket.

Max is gasping, his face flushed. "*Lass mich los!* Get off me!" he says. "I can't breathe!"

"Say sorry," Peter orders.

"They're not your glasses."

"Say sorry!"

"I'll say sorry to Hubert. But not to you. It's got nothing to do with you. You always think you're the center of everything."

Peter catches his breath. "I do not!"

"If you don't get your way, you hate it. You didn't even go home when your mother called you. And that's not even your bike – it's Hubert's. I bet as soon as you get the chance you'll leave us here and move away and you won't think about us again. You think you're such a hero. But you're not. You're a rat."

Peter says nothing, his knees digging into Max's shoulders. Finally he hops off him.

The boys stare at each other, before Max turns and runs off, leaving Peter standing in the street feeling angry and bewildered.

Opa
GRANDFATHER

"Wash your hands, *bitte*," Peter's grandmother tells him when he gets home.

"They're clean," Peter says.

"*Aber jetzt!* Now!" his oma orders.

Peter does as he's told and returns to take a seat at the kitchen table next to his grandfather. He's reading the newspaper as usual. Oma puts a plate of bean salad and potatoes in front of him. She takes her seat and pours herself a beer.

"Your mother was not very happy with you," she says to Peter.

He shrugs. "So what's new? But I wasn't doing anything wrong, just playing in the street."

"That's what I told her," Oma says, taking a sip from her glass. "Children need to be outside, running and climbing and riding – that's how they grow strong. But there'll be no back talk from you while I'm in charge."

Peter nods. He always thinks that Oma looks as though she could be out there running, and climbing. Looking after Opa keeps her fit. And her rosy cheeks and her ice-blue eyes make her seem much younger than she is. But Opa has lost weight since he had a stroke earlier that year. They have to help him with almost everything.

"Oma, are Mutti and Vati serious about moving to the West?"

"I believe so," Oma tells him. "If you ask me, I think we should just stay put. Why would I want to move to the West and have to start all over again? How can that be a better life? I don't want to be a refugee in my own city."

Opa looks up. Peter can tell that he's annoyed with Oma. His face is scrunched up more than usual. So often these days his eyes and big bushy eyebrows have to do the talking for him. Words are hard for him – they come out sounding all mushy and slurred, so he doesn't often talk.

"*Wir gehen!* We'll go!" he slurs. He bangs his fist on

the table and tips his plate on himself.

"Oh, *mein Schatz!* My darling!" Oma says. She grabs a cloth and starts wiping up the mess on Opa's shirt. "Look what you've done."

Peter sighs and shrugs at Opa.

I know, he thinks. I know you hate being looked after like a helpless baby.

"Yes, Ernst, my love," says Oma, trying to calm Opa. "We will go. We'll move to the West and all our troubles will disappear."

Peter knows what a stroke is now – when your brain doesn't get enough oxygen and some of the cells that affect your movement or speech die. But he didn't know that the morning he found Opa collapsed and helpless on the floor of his bedroom.

Oma purses her lips at Peter as she sits back down, as if to say, "Let's not get him worked up!"

After dinner, Peter helps Opa into bed. The left side of his upper body is almost useless, and he shuffles when he tries to walk. This is a first for Peter. Usually Oma or his father helps out. Peter places Opa's arm around his neck and lowers him down onto the mattress.

"*Wir gehen*," Opa says again.

"Yes, Opa," Peter says. "When Mutti and Vati get back tomorrow night, they might have found somewhere for us to live in the West."

Peter thinks about what Max said. If his parents go, he'll have to go as well. He tries to imagine leaving Hubert and Max behind. Would that really make him a traitor? A rat?

—

Early the following morning Peter wakes up to a banging on the apartment door. His grandparents are still asleep. When he swings open the door he is surprised to see Hubert standing there.

"They're putting barbed wire up," he says in a panic. "A barbed-wire fence!"

"What? Slow down. What are you talking about?" Peter asks.

"The army! The police! They've put up a barbed-wire fence right through the middle of the city. No one is getting through. They're saying people can't get to the West anymore!"

Der Westen
THE WEST

Peter, Hubert and Herr Ackermann push their way as far as they can into the crowd. Border guards and construction teams are rolling out barbed wire and planting concrete poles.

"This is an anti-Fascist protection barrier," comes a voice blaring from loudspeakers propped on a van. "Please, step back! Go home! If anyone attempts to cross over without the correct papers they will be arrested!"

Army trucks and jeeps roar in with more troops to keep the crowd at bay. Soldiers with big, scary-looking dogs pace up and down along the boundary.

"Judging by the number of armed troops and the

guard dogs, they really mean business," says Herr Ackermann. "Ulbricht said he wouldn't put up a wall! Mark my words, this is just the start. We're trapped."

Peter knows that Walter Ulbricht is the head of the East German state. He's always in the news reports. Just the mention of his name gets Opa riled up.

"But the West can't just let this just happen," says a man standing beside them. "My wife is over there. I need to get to her."

"I'm trying to get to work," says the man next to him. "I'll lose my job if they don't let me through."

Peter turns to Hubert. "My mother and father are over there, and Margrit! Can they come back?" he says, his voice cracking with panic. "Can I go to them?"

Hubert shakes his head. "I don't know."

Peter's breath quickens. I have to do something, he thinks. He runs toward the border checkpoint but doesn't get anywhere near it. A border guard, wearing an olive-colored uniform and a *Kampfgruppe* cloth cap, steps in front of him.

"*Halt!*" he barks. "Don't get yourself in trouble, boy."

Peter looks nervously at the soldier's rifle. "My mother and father are over there. You've got to let me through. Please!"

"No one gets through," snaps the guard. "Step away!"

"No!" cries Peter, and without thinking he bolts past the man and runs toward the barbed wire.

After only a few steps he's tackled by another guard. He hits the ground hard, and the breath is knocked out of him.

He hears the crowd around them boo and jeer.

"He's only a kid! Let him go!" shouts Herr Ackermann, pushing through the crowd behind them, with Hubert close behind.

The guard clasps Peter by his shirt and yanks him to his feet. "Try another stunt like that and we'll lock you up and throw away the key," he growls. "Now go home."

Hubert's father hurriedly pulls Peter away. "Are you trying to get yourself killed?"

Peter looks at Hubert, who seems close to tears. His own face feels flushed and his chest is heaving.

He turns and runs. This time away from the barrier. Peter can hear Hubert calling after him. "Don't do anything stupid, Peter! Be careful."

Stupid? thinks Peter. Stupid is putting up a barrier around a whole section of Berlin. Stupid is stopping people from coming and going in their own city. Stupid is not going with Mutti when she told me to.

Peter runs toward the Brandenburg Gate. Just yesterday his parents and little sister would have driven freely along the road there. Guards might have stopped them to check their papers, but most people would have been able to come and go as they wanted over the border.

When Peter reaches the border crossing, the crowd is huge. He looks up at the gate with its imposing columns and large sculpture on top of a chariot drawn by four horses. It reminds him of a giant pitchfork stuck in the ground with the handle snapped off.

There are even more soldiers on the road here. Everyone on the East Berlin side is eerily quiet, as if they are in shock, stunned into silence. But through the columns over on the west side – just a few hundred meters away – people are shouting and chanting angrily.

There has to be a way through, thinks Peter.

He runs and runs for over an hour – from crossing point to crossing point. But every checkpoint is blocked.

I'll take a train, he thinks, making his way to the Friedrichstrasse train station.

But when he gets there he sees hundreds of people milling around. No one seems to know what to do. The TraPos, the transport police, have blocked the ticket halls and stopped all the trains going to the

West. Standing side by side with guns slung over their shoulders, they are also blocking the entrances to the platforms.

Some bystanders are loud and angry, and the TraPos are busy dealing with people who have been removed from the trains. An elderly woman in front of Peter pleads with one of the officers.

"Let me through," she says. "I need to be with my grandchildren. I'm all alone, and I've traveled for over two hours. Please don't stop me now."

But the officer doesn't listen. He just shoves the lady backward, along with a few other passengers. She stumbles a few steps before regaining her balance.

"Hey!" Peter shouts. He steps forward to help the lady, but a hand from behind grabs him by the shoulder.

"Peter, don't get involved."

Peter turns to see his neighbor Sabine Roeder. She's a university student who lives with her mother, Herta, in the apartment two doors down.

"They've blocked every way through to the West. This is insane," she says. "Let's go."

"My parents are over there," Peter says, falling into step beside her. "When am I going to see them again, Sabine?" His voice sounds small.

"I'm sorry," she says, looking around as if she's

searching for someone. "I don't know. But I do know that I can't live my life here. I'm not going to let bad timing stop me. I'm getting out of here."

"But what about your mother?"

"She wants me to go. Once I'm in the West, I'll find a way to get her over there."

"But how will you get out?" Peter asks, just as a young man strides toward Sabine. He's carrying a bouquet of flowers.

"This is Manfred," says Sabine.

He nods to Peter but is clearly not in the mood for a chat. "You ready?" he says to Sabine, looking nervous.

"Let's go," Sabine says.

They obviously have a plan. This might be my only chance to leave, Peter thinks. "*Bitte*, please, can I come with you?" Peter asks.

Sabine shakes her head. "Go home, Peter."

Sabine and Manfred jog across the street. When they turn the corner, Peter sets out after them.

Halt!
STOP!

Peter shadows Sabine and Manfred until they reach the wall around a small cemetery. They glance back in his direction. Peter ducks behind a parked car, a little Trabant – the most common automobile in the East. Peering over the tiny hood, he sees them walking through the gate.

I know this place, Peter thinks. The cemetery backs onto the border. Manfred and Sabine are making it look as if they are visiting a grave. They're obviously planning to climb over the cemetery wall and cross over into the West that way. It's a brilliant idea.

But then he hears voices behind him. Back down the street, a group of soldiers from the NPA, the

National People's Army, are marching in his direction. They're easy to recognize from their turtle-shell-shaped helmets. And they're serious and stiff, like their shin-high leather boots. There's no time to waste – Peter follows Sabine and Manfred into the cemetery.

The area is dotted with large oak trees and blanketed in overgrown grass and weeds. Dirt paths wind among old cracked headstones and newer, better-cared-for graves.

It doesn't take long for Peter to catch up. He hides behind a tree, right next to a freshly dug grave. There's a pile of soil with a shovel stuck in it right beside the hole, but no coffin and no mourners.

Sabine and Manfred don't seem to have spotted him. He hopes the soldiers haven't either. Ahead, Manfred is helping Sabine to climb over a high brick wall. On the other side is the West. And freedom.

"Halt! Halt!"

Peter turns to see more soldiers running toward them from another entrance to the cemetery.

"Stop! Stop, or we'll shoot!" a soldier shouts.

Sabine pulls herself up to the top of the wall and turns to pull Manfred after her. But as he tries to launch himself up, the soldiers swarm on him and grab him by the ankles.

With a cry, Sabine jumps to the other side, and

Manfred is pulled back down to the ground.

Peter's heart is pounding. If the soldiers spot me they'll arrest me too, he thinks. He slinks down along the trunk of the tree, drops into the grave and crouches there, frozen.

The soldiers drag Manfred right past him. Peter catches a glimpse of Manfred's face as they pass and sees terror in his eyes. Peter holds his breath and stays motionless until he hears the soldiers' voices fade in the distance.

Only then does he realize that he's trapped himself. The grave is way too deep to simply step out of. Peter panics. Now what?

He jumps a couple of times, trying to claw at the top of the grave – but it's useless. He's still a long way from the top.

Peter hears someone approaching and his heart races even faster. One of the soldiers has obviously stayed back, he thinks. If he finds me here, this could end up being my grave! Peter scans the ground and spots a partly buried rock. He picks it up. It's a little larger than his fist.

When the footsteps seem to have passed by, Peter frantically begins digging small holes into one of the hard dirt walls. Standing on his toes he shovels out two holes shoulder-width apart – as high as he can reach – another around the level of his face, and one more at waist-level.

Peter drops the rock. "Here goes," he whispers, wedging his right foot in the hole closest to his waist and pushing up to grab the two highest holes. With as secure a grip as he can manage, he raises his left foot and places it in the next hole up.

Using all the strength he can muster, Peter grits his teeth and propels his body upward. He lunges for the top of the ditch, clutching at a clump of grass and pushing a foot into one of the higher holes.

"Yes!" he sighs, lifting himself out of the grave.

Peter looks up to see a soldier standing only a few graves away. Thankfully the man is facing away from him. He exhales quietly, then springs to his feet and bolts for the entrance.

But then he hears someone following him. "*Halt! Halt!*" cries a man. Big boots are thumping against the ground behind him.

Peter runs faster than he ever has before. Thankfully no new soldiers appear. But he doesn't stop running until he has put the cemetery far behind him.

—

"Thank heavens!" Oma rushes to Peter when he gets home. "Are you all right? We were so worried."

Peter nods, but he doesn't feel all right.

"You're out of breath." Oma hugs him tightly. "I can't believe the government has done this to us. Sit down and I'll get you a drink."

Peter joins Opa at the kitchen table. Opa is shaking his head as he listens to the reports coming from the West on the radio. He's clearly upset. He always said something like this would happen – that the Communist government would take away their rights. That something bad would happen. He mutters as the news crackles through the tiny speakers. He places his shaking hand on Peter's wrist.

Peter can't look at him. He knows if he does, he might not be able to control the emotions surging up inside of him.

Just as Oma hands Peter a glass of water there's a knock at the door. Oma opens it cautiously. It's Sabine's mother, Herta Roeder.

"Oh, Frieda," she says to Oma. "This is terrible. I've just come from visiting my friend. I've heard that the people who live in the apartments running along the border are going to be kicked out of their homes."

"What?" gasps Oma.

"Why?" asks Peter, shocked.

"The rear of the buildings are here in the East," says Frau Roeder, "but the front of the buildings are in the West."

"Like Bernauerstrasse?" says Oma.

Frau Roeder nods. "There's talk that the police are going to raid the apartments, evict the residents and brick up all the windows and doors. What's this world coming to? I hope Sabine and Manfred are all right. I hope they made it across!"

Peter knows he will have to tell her, but he doesn't know how. He looks up to see Opa staring at him. His opa knows him too well – he can tell that Peter knows something.

"I told them it would be dangerous, but you know Sabine, and Manfred for that matter, when they set their minds to something . . ."

"Sabine got through," Peter blurts out. "But Manfred didn't. I'm so sorry, Frau Roeder. He's been arrested."

Niemandem trauen
DON'T TRUST ANYONE

When Peter and Oma arrive at the Invalidenstrasse checkpoint, Peter sees that the guards and the police, all holding assault rifles, have now pushed the crowds farther back from the border. They hurry people along if they try to stop and look over. Peter and Oma walk slowly. There are so many people on the western side waving and calling out.

Peter scans the masses on the other side of the barbed wire. Then he spots a woman in the distance. The sun is setting behind her and there's a hazy glare in the sky so it's hard to tell, but he thinks it could be his mother.

Then the light shifts. "That's her!" he tells Oma.

"It's Mutti! And there's Vatti. He's just stepped up beside her, and he's holding Margrit."

He waves to them. Oma waves. But Peter's parents don't seem to see them in the crowd. Peter wants to shout to them, but he knows they're too far away and he doesn't want to draw any attention from the guards.

His mother turns and drops her head onto his father's chest. Even from this far away Peter can see that she's shaking, crying. Peter's chest tightens. He feels hopeless and lost and afraid. He turns and sees tears streaming down Oma's face. She wipes them away quickly when she notices Peter looking at her.

"Let's go!" she says, turning abruptly.

"But we just got here," Peter says.

"There's nothing we can do. There's nothing any of us can do. They'll send us away soon anyway. And we must get back to Opa."

Peter waves one more time to his parents and sister. He doesn't want to take his eyes off them. But Oma has already walked on. Peter tells himself that he's not going to cry. He hears Max's voice in his head: "You didn't even go home when your mother called you. You'll move away, leave us here, and never think about us again. You think you're such a hero. But you're not. You're a rat."

Well, I'm stuck here now, Peter thinks, waving one more time to his family before running after Oma. But I'd rather be a traitor.

Oma doesn't talk on the way home. She's marching ahead at a quick pace. Just before they reach the entrance of their building she stops abruptly and turns to Peter.

"Now I want you to listen to me very carefully," she says sternly, her face hard. "If you have any thoughts at all – even the slightest inkling – of trying to escape to the West, put them right out of your head. This government means business. Never forget what happened here during the last war."

Peter bites his bottom lip, feeling afraid. The war ended before he was born and he has never heard his Oma talk about it before.

"Governments like this one kill people who don't agree with them. And those soldiers at the border will shoot you without even thinking about it because it's their job."

Peter starts to turn his face away from her, but she grabs it tightly, squeezing his cheeks.

"Listen, Manfred's family might never see him again. I'm sure he's been locked away in a cell, maybe chained up like a dog. He had his whole life ahead of him and now has nothing. And, what's worse, the silly *Dummkopf* has drawn the attention of the Stasi, the secret police, to his family and to our building too. Mark my words. We haven't seen the end of this."

But Peter doesn't think Sabine and Manfred are silly. They seem brave to him.

"You're all we've got now," Oma says. "And we love you very much. So keep your mouth shut. Don't trust anyone. And promise me you won't do anything *dämlich*!"

Peter nods. "Yes, Oma," he says. But behind his back he crosses his fingers. It depends what you mean by "idiotic," he thinks.

—

Later that night, as Peter helps his opa get into bed, a thought crosses his mind. Opa has been a prisoner before – in the First World War when he was a young man.

"Opa," he says. "When you were in the prison camp, did you ever try to escape?"

Opa squints his eyes and then nods.

"Really?"

Opa nods again. Peter doesn't know much about the horrors Opa experienced in the Soviet camps. But he knows that lots of Germans didn't survive them. And he knows that's why Opa detests the government and why moving to the West can't come soon enough for him.

His parents would never tell Peter any details about what happened to Opa. His father had only said, "Think of evil, and then multiply it by a hundred. That's how bad it was." Peter has never had the courage to ask Opa about it before.

"Will you tell me the story?" Peter asks.

Before Opa can attempt an answer, Oma walks into the room.

"*Gute Nacht*, Peter," she says. "Time for bed. It's been an emotional day for all of us."

Peter sighs heavily as he leaves his grandparents and goes to the bedroom he shared with his family. He sits on his bed, but he's in no mood for sleeping. His mind is spinning.

He looks at his parents' bed and at Margrit's bed, which is pushed up against his. Six people living in a two-bedroom apartment had felt crowded, but now Peter feels so alone. He looks forlornly at the stuffed toys on Margrit's pillow. One is a bear, the other a duck.

He loves his oma and opa, but how can he live without Margrit and his parents?

Suddenly he has a brilliant idea that pushes his sadness aside. He lunges forward and grabs the toy duck.

That's it, he thinks. The river! I'll swim across to the West.

Der Fluss
THE RIVER

The cuckoo clock ticks loudly in the hallway – it's a little after midnight. Peter tiptoes past his grandparents' bedroom. Their door is ajar. He hears Opa snoring, and turns to see them snuggled into each other. Oma has her arm flung over Opa.

Peter sighs. Opa was a prisoner of war in an actual prison and he tried to escape, he tells himself, hurrying toward the front door. There's no way I'm going to give up and be a prisoner in my own city.

When Peter steps outside, he edges along the wall of his building and down the street, hiding in doorways whenever a car or army jeep drives by.

When he reaches the district of Friedrichshain,

he makes his way toward the River Spree. The Spree snakes through the city of Berlin, but this part of the river forms a natural border between the East and the West.

On the other side of the river Peter can see the district of Kreuzberg, which is in the West. Over there he sees lights twinkling and hears the sounds of life: a car door slamming, laughter echoing, music blaring from an open window. On his side it's still, stark and ghostly. The wide streets are empty and most of the lights are out.

Everyone is hidden away – in our prison-cell apartments, Peter thinks, as he slips in behind a clump of reeds. He takes a moment to catch his breath. He's sweating. It's taken almost an hour from his home in the neighborhood of Mitte to get here.

Peter scopes out the area. Visibility is low – he can just make out the riverbank on the other side. It's about a hundred and fifty meters away. The river has a strong current, but he can definitely swim the distance.

Peter thinks back to when he was swimming last summer. When he was doing his best cannonballs with Hubert and Max, he couldn't have known that his next swim would be so dangerous.

"Why did dumb politics have to get between me

and my friends?" he mutters.

Peter kicks off his shoes and takes off his shirt. He doesn't want anything to drag him down or make it harder to swim across the current.

He will have to swim in a way that won't draw attention. That means minimal splashing. Best if I do breaststroke, he thinks. It's slower, but I have to cross this river like a water rat – not a ripple in sight.

As Peter steps toward the river's edge, there's a rustle in the tall reeds. Peter thinks the worst – a border guard? A border guard's ferocious dog? Both?

"Who are you?" comes a shaky whisper, startling Peter.

A young man emerges from the darkness. He's barefoot and he doesn't look much older than Sabine and Manfred.

"Are you going to swim across too?" he asks, starting to unbutton his shirt. "My fiancé's over there, and there's no way I'm going to live here without her."

The young man is wearing shorts under his trousers. He pushes past Peter.

"I don't think we should swim together," he adds, wading in waist deep. "Two of us will be spotted more easily than one. The river patrol boat cruised by here about five minutes ago – downstream. You'll just have to wait."

"Why should I?" says Peter, defiantly. "My family is over there. I'll go first."

"No, you won't. I've been waiting hours for the right time. Get in line, kid."

The young man dives into the water and starts swimming as fast as he can.

Peter grabs his shoes and shirt. He will have to look for another spot to enter the water. He looks out at the river and sees that the young man is about halfway across. But just then he hears the sound of an engine approaching fast from around the bend. It's the river police!

Peter drops to the ground and peers through the reeds. The patrol boat beams a huge spotlight onto the young man.

"*Halt! Halt!*" the police shout.

The young man dives below the surface.

Peter's entire body is frozen with fear. He imagines what it would be like to be in that cold water, lit up by a spotlight, with police shouting at him.

The patrol boat glides to where the man disappeared beneath the surface. There is no sign of him now. There's a lot of shouting from the police on board the boat, and then . . . they fire their guns, spraying bullets into the water.

Peter's heart feels as if it's been shoved into his

throat. He can hardly breathe. He wants to run but can't move. He closes his eyes and covers his ears to block out the terrifying gunshots.

Peter stays as still as a statue for a very long time, shivering in the darkness. Even after the patrol boat's motor fades into the distance, his mind is in overload, his hands trembling, his heart still beating furiously. He tells himself that the young man must have swum underwater to the other side. That the bullets missed him. That he hasn't been shot, or caught and taken away. That he has made it to safety.

But is that possible?

It's not until dawn that Peter's nerves calm down. He checks to see that no one is around, stumbles to his feet, and runs.

When he gets home, Oma and Opa are still asleep. He sneaks back into his bedroom, grabs Margrit's soft toy duck, jumps under the covers, and holds it tightly.

"If I'm going to escape," he whispers into his pillow, "I've got to be a whole lot smarter than that."

Tauben
PIGEONS

"We thought you were going to sleep all day," says Oma, as Peter enters the kitchen and grabs a couple of pieces of Filinchen crispbread, one of his favorite snacks. He heads for the door.

"Where are you going?" Oma asks.

"I'm going back to the checkpoint. Hopefully I can see them again," says Peter.

"Sit down," orders Oma. "I'll fry you an egg first."

Peter sighs and sits down at the table next to Opa, who is having coffee and is chewing on a Ketwurst, a hot dog with ketchup.

Peter half smiles at him, but he's not in the mood to talk. He can't stop thinking about the young man in the river. He chews his fingernails as Oma cracks an egg in the frying pan.

"There you go," she says, placing Peter's breakfast in front of him. When she leaves the room, Opa bites off a piece of hot dog and spits it at him to get his attention.

"Opa! What are you doing? That's disgusting!" Peter says.

Opa grunts at him. He slurs a couple of words that Peter doesn't catch.

"Slow down," Peter says, starting to scoff down the fried egg. "Or I can't understand."

"*Hab' dich gesehen!*" Opa slurs. "Saw you!"

Peter stops eating. He heard it clearly this time. He looks up at his opa.

"You saw me?" he whispers, looking back to make sure Oma isn't in earshot. She isn't. She's in her bedroom. "You mean last night?"

Opa nods. "*Ent . . . flie . . . hen.* Es . . . cape."

Peter pauses. He promised Oma he wouldn't even consider trying to escape to the West. Would Opa tell her? He hesitates. But Opa spits more Ketwurst at him.

"Stop that, will you? How much do you have in there?"

Opa raises his eyebrows.

"All right, all right," Peter says, leaning into him.

36

But before he can say anything else, Oma steps back into the room.

"What are you two whispering about?" she says.

"Nothing!" says Peter. "Opa has Ketwurst stuck in his teeth. So what are we going to do?"

"About food stuck in Opa's teeth?"

"No! About getting to the West."

"I'm not sure what any of us can do," says Oma. "But I'm going to visit the visa office. Perhaps they might make some arrangements for families that have been separated."

"Has Mutti called us?" asks Peter. They don't have a telephone in their apartment, but Frau Roeder does. He knows his mother will try to call there if she can.

"Frau Roeder spends all day by the phone, waiting for Sabine to call. Or for Manfred's father to call with information. But no one knows what has happened to him," Oma tells Peter. "She said your mother tried to call yesterday, but the operator was having problems making the connection, or so they said. I can only imagine how many divided families like us are trying to make contact."

Peter wants so badly to hear his parents' voices and to ask them what he should do. "Can we call Vatti's work?" he asks.

"We'll try tomorrow, although we may not get

through, as I'm sure Frau Roeder's phone will be tapped. She's the mother of a deserter now, and the Stasi will be monitoring all calls coming from the West in any case. It's probably a good thing your parents didn't get through to us – for now."

Peter sighs. He has learned how dangerous trying to escape can be, but Oma is making him feel that staying is dangerous too.

—

At Invalidenstrasse, where Peter last saw his parents and sister, he watches the guards keeping people away from the barbed-wire barrier. Construction teams have arrived and they're building an actual wall – mortaring bricks into place.

Peter scans the crowd over on the west side. He doesn't see his family.

Perhaps they've just decided to get on with their lives without me, he thinks glumly. He wonders where they will live in the West. Maybe they're staying at one of the transit refugee camps – like the one called Marienfelde, he thinks. Oma had pointed out a photograph of that camp in the newspaper and said it would be such an awful thing to go through that process – to be herded about like cattle.

Peter hopes his family is staying with friends or one of his father's colleagues from the cinema house where he works. Peter hadn't really paid attention to the details of his father's work before, but he wishes he had.

Peter turns and walks aimlessly along the wide streets. It's an overcast day and low-hanging clouds blend in with the gray of the concrete slab buildings and the asphalt roads. Peter approaches the street Frau Roeder had told them about – where the apartment buildings sit right on the border. The front doors and facades of the buildings open to the West, but the rest of the apartment building is in the East. Peter thinks of the residents and how nervous they must be, wondering if tomorrow they'll have a roof over their heads. At least Opa, Oma and I still have a home, he thinks.

When Peter is about a block away from the border buildings, he notices a handful of brave people protesting – mostly university students. They're chanting political slogans that Peter doesn't really understand.

"This is absurd." Peter overhears a couple of students as they pass him on their way to join the protesters. "I heard the State is planning to bulldoze the apartment buildings. How can they do that? The world is crazy."

Peter nods. The world is crazy!

He looks up and sees three pigeons in the sky flying over the western part of the city. Those birds have more freedom than we do now, he thinks. They can leave whenever they want.

Peter watches the pigeons. They fly in sync, circling over the same area. They don't look like common street pigeons that fly in all directions looking for scraps. Peter keeps his eye on the three as they head his way.

The protesters continue to chant as more and more of them arrive.

The birds circle the rooftop of an apartment building that backs onto one of the border buildings. One by one the pigeons come in for a landing and then disappear from view.

Peter is curious. He runs over to the front of the building, steps through the main entrance and races up the stairwell. It looks just like his family's apartment building. Halfway up, he almost collides with a girl about his age racing down the steps.

"Hey, watch it!" she snaps, looking back over her shoulder at Peter.

Reaching the top floor Peter climbs a final, short set of stairs that lead to the rooftop. He steps out. No one is around. He looks for the pigeons. They are nowhere in sight, but there is a small pigeon coop in the center of the roof. It's a basic construction of chicken wire and wooden boxes stacked on top of each other.

Peter makes his way across to the edge of the roof and looks west. There's a very narrow street, more of a lane, running between the other rooftop and the one he's standing on.

He peers over the ledge and looks down. He starts feeling slightly dizzy and wobbles a step back – it's a long drop. He sighs.

"What are you doing?" comes a voice from behind him.

Fragen
QUESTIONS

Peter whips around to see an older boy standing there – he's maybe fifteen, with jet-black hair that's slicked back like Elvis Presley's. He's wearing a woolen trench coat – in the height of summer.

"I'm not doing anything," says Peter. "Just looking."

"At what?"

"Why does it matter to you?" says Peter.

But instead of answering him, the boy looks down at his coat. "Wolfgang!" he says. "Shush! Ludwig, leave Wolfgang alone."

Peter starts to edge away. Is the boy talking to himself?

Suddenly the boy digs deep into his coat pockets.

To Peter's surprise, he pulls out three pigeons – two from one pocket and one from the other. Two of them flap onto the ground and toddle around his feet. He pats the third pigeon on the back. "That's enough from you, Felix," he says.

"Hey, are they the pigeons I saw circling in the sky?" Peter asks him excitedly. "They're yours?"

The boy nods.

"What sort of pigeons are they?"

"Homing pigeons," the boy says, dropping the third pigeon gently on the ground, "a special breed. They're trained to always come back to their home base. During the war they were used to send secret messages."

"Do you use them to send secret notes?" Peter asks curiously.

"No," snaps the teenager, suddenly impatient. "I just look after them. I was standing here a while before you noticed me. Were you looking at that dumb barrier on the border?"

Peter hesitates, but who else is he going to talk to about it all? He's not sure when he'll see Hubert next and wonders if he's even friends with Max anymore. Before he knows it, he's blurting out his whole story to this stranger.

"And now I'm stuck here with my opa and oma,"

he says breathlessly. "My oma says I shouldn't try to escape to the West because they'll shoot me. And last night I actually saw someone get shot while trying to swim across the river. Well, he might have been shot. They fired at him. But that's not going to stop me. I actually have another idea about how to escape – a great escape plan. It just came to me!"

Peter feels a bit overwhelmed and to his surprise feels a lump in his throat. His face feels flushed, and he's worried he's said too much.

"Hey, relax. Take a breath," says the boy. Then he digs into another pocket and pulls out a handful of birdseed. "Put out your hand. Here."

He puts some seed into Peter's hand, then whistles sharply. The pigeons flap up to him and perch themselves on his forearms.

The boy puts his arm next to Peter's. One of the pigeons hops onto Peter's wrist and begins to peck at the seed in his open palm. Peter feels his breathing calm down.

"Sorry about your family," the boy adds. "This city's messed up. This country's messed up. The whole world is messed up. They've messed it up for all of us."

"They?" says Peter, gently stroking the pigeon. Its feathers are so soft and smooth.

"Adults. Adults mess everything up."

Peter contemplates that for a moment as they silently watch the pigeons eat.

"I'm Otto," says the boy.

"Peter," says Peter.

"Felix really likes you, Peter."

"You said you look after them. Who owns them?" Peter asks.

"More questions," says Otto, but he's smiling. "Their owner used to live here, but now he's stuck in the West, so I guess they are mine now. He was only going over there for a couple of weeks."

"Can you take the pigeons back to your home?"

"I can't. It's not easy to re-home a homing pigeon," Otto says. "They'll just keep flying back here."

"What are their names again?" Peter asks.

"That one is Wolfgang. He's named after Wolfgang Amadeus Mozart. And this plucky guy is Ludwig, after Ludwig van Beethoven. And the smallest one, the one you're holding, is Felix, after Felix Mendelssohn. The old man loves classical music – and he named these three after his favorite composers. They're sort of like his kids."

"So these birds are your adopted children now," says Peter earnestly.

"*Das ist lustig!*" Otto says. "That's funny! I guess they are. So tell me more about your great escape."

45

"Well, it came to me when I was watching these three in the sky. I was thinking if I had wings I could take a running jump off this roof and fly over onto the rooftop of that building. And then off that rooftop and into the West. Brilliant, right?"

Fliegen
FLYING

Otto laughs so much it sets off a coughing fit.

Peter feels embarrassed. He's annoyed by Otto's response.

"Fly?" Otto finally manages to say. "That's a good one."

"It wasn't a joke," Peter says.

Otto snorts a couple more times before he regains his composure. He takes Felix from Peter and moves back toward the coop, cradling all three pigeons.

Peter makes a move back toward the stairwell. He isn't going to stick around just to be made fun of.

"Come on, you really didn't think you could fly?" Otto calls after him as he places the pigeons in the pen. "Don't you think that if it were as simple as strapping on some homemade wings we would all be flying by now? You know basic biology, don't you?"

"No, but I suppose you do," Peter snaps defensively.

"Yeah, I do," Otto says. "Birds have special air sacs connected to their lungs that help them fly. They also have a lightweight skeletal system – their bones are hollow. And their wingspan and wing muscles are huge in proportion to their body size."

Peter stops and turns.

"Well, um, I didn't actually mean *flying*, flying," he says in his own defense, pretending he knew that all along. "I meant more like, you know, making a set of wings and gliding across."

Otto considers the idea. "Possibly," he says. "If you have a strong headwind in your favor and it lifts you. But you still wouldn't go very far. You'd still be too heavy. You'd be more likely to fall to your death. *Splat!*"

"But we're slightly higher than that building over there. So if I ran fast enough, couldn't I create enough of a lift to make it?"

Otto shrugs. "Hey, if you want to take that risk, who am I to stop you?"

"Well, I just might," Peter says defiantly.

"Well, good for you," Otto snaps back. "How would

you build yourself a pair of wings anyway?"

Peter knows that Otto is just humoring him, but he's sticking by his idea, as crazy and dangerous as it sounds.

"Cardboard, I guess," he replies honestly.

"*Nein*. Not strong enough," says Otto. "And you wouldn't get any lift."

"Feathers on a wire frame?"

"You'd need to collect a lot of feathers. Thousands and thousands!"

"Well, I could do that," Peter declares. "Yes, that's what I'm going to do."

Otto stares at Peter with a slight smile.

"There's no way feathers are going to work, but I might have another idea," he says. "I'll help you make these wings on one condition. I live in Prenzlauer Berg with my family, so you take care of the pigeons when I can't. And if I'm ever not around, they're your responsibility. Deal?"

It doesn't take Peter long to respond.

"*Abgemacht!* It's a deal!" he says, shaking Otto's hand.

Ein Mädchen
A GIRL

As Peter weaves past other pedestrians he notices a girl walking on the other side of the street. It's hard to miss her – her fiery red hair stands out against the gray concrete buildings behind her. He picks up his pace. But so does she. When he slows down, she slows down.

She's following me, Peter thinks. But why? Maybe she's got something to do with the secret police Oma was talking about? The Stasi?

Peter begins to jog and when he glances across the street she isn't there. But then he spots her again. On his side of the street, about twenty meters directly behind him. She seems familiar. It finally dawns on

Peter that she's the girl from the stairwell.

Right, enough of this, Peter thinks, and he launches into a sprint. There's no way she'll keep up with me!

Peter bolts and makes a sharp left into Gartenstrasse. He lengthens his stride and runs a couple more blocks. When he turns right into Invalidenstrasse, he slows down to a jog and looks back over his shoulder.

"Lost her," he pants. But he jogs the rest of the way home anyway. When he gets back, his face feels flushed.

"What have you been up to?" Oma says, as Peter steps up next to her at the kitchen sink, grabs a glass and fills it with water from the faucet.

"Just running," he says in between gulps.

"Did you see your parents and sister at the checkpoint?"

He shakes his head. Something outside the window has caught his eye. There on the street, looking up in his direction, is that girl.

Peter can't believe it. He runs out of the apartment, with Oma calling out after him. "Peter! *Was ist los?* What's going on?"

When he charges out of the building onto the street the girl is gone. Peter whips his head from side to side. She's nowhere to be seen.

"Hey, Peter!" It's Hubert riding up to him on his bike.

"My mother said you can have dinner with us tonight," he says excitedly. But then he remembers the reason his mother invited Peter and frowns. "She said you must be . . . well, you know, um, sad, well, maybe not sad, but kind of down since –"

"Yes, of course I'll come," says Peter, cutting Hubert off. "Did you see a girl, with red hair, just now?"

"No. Why?"

"Doesn't matter," Peter sighs. Just then he spots Max and a couple of older boys he doesn't know walking their way.

"Hi, Hubert!" Max calls out. Then he notices Peter. "Hi, traitor! I heard your family deserted to the West. And, look . . . you're stuck here. Too bad."

"Just ignore him," Hubert mutters to Peter.

But Peter is seething. And he's already marching toward the boys, with gritted teeth and clenched fists.

"Come on!" Max taunts. "*Du traust dich ja nicht!* I dare you!"

"Max!" Hubert calls. "This is stupid." He drops his bike and runs up behind Peter. "Don't worry about them," he says. "Think about it. There are three of them and they're all bigger than us. Just walk away."

"I bet this is killing you," Max says, trying to

provoke Peter. "You want to be with your mama, but you can't! Boo-hoo. Not the hero now, are you, rat?"

Peter's entire body tenses up when he sees Max grinning and glancing back at his friends, who all have the same arrogant look.

"That's it!" Peter growls, and he charges at Max. But all three boys lunge forward and tackle him to the ground. In the scuffle they begin punching him.

Peter curls up in a ball. Hubert tries to help, but is pushed aside by Max. It feels as though Peter is hurting all over. Then he feels Max's fist connect with his cheek with a flash of pain.

"*Lasst ihn los!*" Someone is yelling from somewhere close by. "Get off him now!"

With his eye starting to swell up and his face half pressed into the pavement, Peter catches sight of Oma shuffling really fast toward them. She's wielding a wooden spoon and looking really fearsome.

She's the best, Peter thinks. The next second she's there and she's smacking Max and his friends with the wooden spoon.

Two men walking by rush to Oma's side. The three boys stop and stumble backward and then bolt down the street.

The adults help Peter to his feet. His nose is bloody and his right cheek and eye feel bruised and swollen.

His world has been turned upside down.

Why can't it be like it used to be? he thinks, now feeling embarrassed as Oma pulls him in toward her and hugs him tightly.

Geld
MONEY

"*Sehr lecker*, Frau Ackermann! This Sülze is very tasty," Peter says.

"Thank you, Peter," says Hubert's mother. She's always been proud of her jellied meat loaf with Spree pickles and onions. "I was thinking of making Königsberger Klopse, meatballs and boiled potatoes, but this is better for such a warm summer's evening."

For the first time since his parents left, Peter feels comforted and safe, even though the right side of his face is black-and-blue. It's nice to be sitting around a full table. Hubert is the middle child in his family. He has two brothers. Ralf is eighteen and Paul is five, the same age as Margrit.

Reaching for another piece of meat loaf and hearing Hubert tease his little brother, Peter feels as if life has almost returned to normal. But then Hubert's father reminds him that it hasn't.

"Still no word from your parents?" Herr Ackermann asks. "I'm sure they must be beside themselves."

Peter shakes his head.

Ralf has obviously been waiting the whole time for the subject to come up. "So many families have been separated," he says. "Why hasn't the Bundesrepublik or America stepped in to help us? Don't they care?"

Hubert's mother shifts awkwardly in her chair and looks apologetically at Peter.

"We'll miss out on so many things because of this stupid wall," Ralf continues. "People who speak their mind are being arrested or disappearing. A couple of my old friends have already given up. They're spouting communist propaganda and joining the FDJ, the Free German Youth. There's nothing 'free' about it! We can't just sit around and do nothing – that's never been my way. We have to take a stand!"

"Please, Ralf, enough," Hubert's mother says. "Let Peter enjoy his meal. He's had a lot to deal with and this is unfair on him."

"Yes, sorry, Peter," says Ralf. "I'm sorry that you

and thousands of others like you find yourselves in this despicable situation. I know you must be angry, if not angrier than me. So we can't sit back and –"

"Ralf!" Herr Ackermann says, raising his voice. "Stop. Enough politics for now."

"Mutti," says Hubert. "Can Peter and I be excused? I want to show him my new books for school."

Hubert's mother nods. Peter makes a face. Schoolbooks? he thinks. The new school year will be starting soon, in another couple of weeks. Without his parents, he hasn't organized anything.

Peter follows Hubert into his bedroom.

"So . . . schoolbooks, really?" he says.

"No, of course not!" snorts Hubert. "I wanted to show you these."

Hubert pulls a pair of jeans out of the bottom drawer of his small cupboard. He's grinning.

"Remember Rainer, the kid who always wanted to come swimming with us, but his mother wouldn't let him?"

Peter nods.

"Well, his cousins in America gave him these. Rainer and his family moved to the West a week ago and he said I could have them. He can get more over there. *Toll, nicht wahr?* Great, right? Real American jeans."

Peter's impressed. Most adults he knows don't like jeans. He knows of kids at his school who were sent home for wearing them. And some places have even banned any young people who wear them.

"I think these could be worth something, don't you? Especially now that the barrier has gone up," Hubert adds excitedly. "I think I could make some good money selling them."

Peter had always felt annoyed that they couldn't have the same things as people in the West. You couldn't buy things like bananas, but you could get them over the border. But now he doesn't care about not having all the latest toys and clothes, or sweets and fruit. What did any of that matter when you don't have your family?

Hubert stops talking about jeans. "Sorry," he says, tossing them onto his bed. "Mutti says things are probably tough for you and your grandparents, so I want you to have this." Hubert opens the top drawer and takes out some money. He holds it out.

"Here. That's nine marks," he says. "I've been collecting bottles, paper and metal scraps and taking them to the recycling centers."

Recycling collection centers are everywhere in Peter's neighborhood. All the kids make money collecting aerosol cans, books and even used camera film, but nine marks is pretty impressive.

"Why are you giving me this?" he asks.

"Because who's going to make money now that your parents are gone?" he replies. "Your opa can't work. And your oma may be great at wielding wooden spoons, but she doesn't have a job. My father says that the government provides a pension for old people, which I suppose is good, but it won't be much . . . I thought this could help you right now."

Peter is taken aback. Partly because he hates feeling like his family needs charity, but mostly because he hadn't really thought about what was going to happen next, about how he and Oma and Opa were going to live. His mother and father had both worked, and he's never had to think about money before.

"We don't need help," he says defensively. "I can collect bottles too. Lots, if I have to!"

"Sorry, I didn't mean . . ." Hubert stammers.

"Forget about it," says Peter, realizing how ungrateful he must sound. Hubert is a good friend and Peter knows he would do the same thing if their situations were reversed. "I'll be fine."

But he wonders if they will be.

Federn

FEATHERS

Early the following morning Peter is back on the rooftop. Every morning for a week, while Otto is at work, Peter has agreed to feed Wolfgang, Ludwig and Felix and release them from the coop to let them fly for a bit. In the afternoons the boys would meet to work on the plan.

Peter takes a bag of seeds out of his pocket and scatters them on the floor of the coop. The pigeons peck at the feed, their heads frantically bobbing up and down. Once they're done eating, Peter opens the coop and shoos them out. They flap, flutter and take to the sky. First Wolfgang, then Ludwig and finally little Felix.

Peter smiles as he watches them come together and circle above, flying side by side, twisting and turning as if they are putting on an aerial show just for him.

As the pigeons soar among the low-hanging clouds Peter begins to imagine what his homemade wings will look like. He pictures them with feathers, but knows Otto thinks that's a crazy idea. He's right, he thinks. Everyone could fly if it were as simple as sticking a bunch of feathers together. What was I thinking?

He wonders what Otto has in mind.

Peter hears the door to the rooftop creak. He turns to see the redheaded girl looking at him.

"Hey!" he calls out to her. She must live in one of these apartments, Peter thinks.

"What are you doing?" the girl asks.

"Were you trying to sneak up on me?" Peter says. "Why did you follow me home the other day? Who are you?"

"I was going to ask you the same thing," says the girl, crossing her arms. "What are you doing in my building? Why are you feeding Herr Weber's pigeons? Who are you working for?"

"I'm not working for anyone," Peter exclaims. "You ask plenty of questions, but you still haven't answered mine. Who are you? Why have you been following me?"

"I'm just making sure you're not going to be any trouble," says the girl. "And clearly you're not."

"Trouble? What do you mean?" asks Peter.

"Trouble, as in somebody who works for the government or the police," the girl exclaims. "Spying on people. Ready to rat them out."

"Why? Are you planning to escape?" Peter asks.

"You mean, like you?" she says. "Am I right?"

"No!" says Peter. "But . . . what makes you think that I want to?"

The girl shrugs. "I heard what that *frecher Junge*, that mean boy, said to you the other day. He called you a traitor before he beat you up."

"You were there?" Peter asks. "I thought you were gone when I came out on the street."

"I'm just good at hiding and making myself invisible." She grins. "Even with this wild hair of mine. So . . . your family are in the West, and I bet you'll do anything to join them, right?"

Fernsprecher
TELEPHONE

The girl's name is Elke. "So what's your plan then?" she asks. "And what's your name?"

"It's Peter. And even if I had a plan, I wouldn't tell you," Peter says. "And I don't think that if you were planning an escape to the West you would tell me either, right?"

Elke doesn't answer.

"Thought so," Peter says. But he's beginning to wonder whether Elke is in the same situation as he is. "So you've been separated from your family too, then?"

"My father is over there. My mother and I were planning to join him the day the barbed wire went up."

Peter replays what Oma said to him: "Keep your

mouth shut and don't trust anyone!" He has probably said too much to Elke already.

While they are talking the pigeons return to the rooftop. Peter picks them up gently and places them back in their coop, then tells Elke that he has to leave.

"*Tschüss*," he says, hoping that she won't be there in the afternoon when he meets up with Otto. "Bye!"

—

"Where have you been?" Oma asks. "Your mother telephoned!"

"What? When?" Peter says, feeling as if he has been punched again by one of Max's thugs.

"Half an hour ago. She's going to call again in ten minutes. I wasn't sure if you were going to get back in time. *Beeil dich!* Hurry! Let's go over to Frau Roeder's."

They walk quickly down the hall to the apartment.

"Oh, Peter, you made it," Frau Roeder says as she leads them to the telephone table in the hallway. "Here . . . sit down."

Peter takes a seat. As he waits for his mother's call, he hears the two women talking quietly in the kitchen.

"Sabine hasn't called, but I have news of Manfred," Frau Roeder says, her voice sounding fragile. "His father told me that he could be imprisoned for up to two years for the crime of *Republikflucht* – attempting to escape from the republic. No one is allowed to see him. Oh, Frieda – I'm sure they are watching my every movement now. Did you notice two men seated in a car parked right outside our building? They're not from this neighborhood, that's for sure. I don't know what to do." She sounds close to tears. "I'm going to stay with my sister in Leipzig for a while. Here's a key. *Bitte*, if I don't come back take whatever you need of mine. I'd rather you have my things, dear friend."

"But, Herta, what do you mean if you don't come back? What about your work?" says Oma.

The telephone rings loudly, startling the three of them. Peter takes a deep breath and picks up the handset.

"Hello?" he says. At first all he can hear is a series of clicks.

"Please hold," says the operator. "We're connecting you now."

Peter waits several seconds, but it feels like an eternity. Finally he hears a faint voice through the crackling connection.

"Hello? Peter?" says his mother.

Die Mauer
THE WALL

Peter and Oma return to their apartment. Peter's stomach is churning as he sits down at the table next to Opa.

He replays the short, fragmented conversation: his mother unable to control her tears, telling him she loves him. "Don't you worry . . . we'll work something out. Let's try to wave to each other again later today around five. This won't last long, it can't . . ."

And then his father telling him that he's the man of the house. Telling him to be strong for Opa and Oma. "We'll work something out," he said. "These heartless bureaucrats –"

And then the line just went dead. As if someone

had intentionally broken the connection.

Peter sits in the kitchen wondering if his mother is still crying over there in the West. Why didn't I say more? he thinks. I should've said more!

Peter glances up at Opa, who always knows what he's thinking. Opa extends his trembling hand, the one not paralyzed by the stroke, and places something on Peter's forearm. It's a rubber spider.

Opa winks and rolls his eyes toward Oma. She has her back to them and is taking cups out of the cupboard. Peter knows what his opa is up to. He's trying to cheer him up. They've played this trick on Oma before – she's terrified of spiders.

Peter places the fake spider on Oma's chair. Oma brings the cups to the table, pours the tea, sits the kettle back on the stove, and returns to her seat – then squeals at the top of her lungs.

Peter and Opa burst out laughing.

"Oh! You silly boys!" she cries. "Really? Jokes? At a time like this?" But in the end she laughs too.

Peter places his hand on Opa's hand and whispers, "*Danke schön*, Opa! Thank you!"

Opa winks back.

"Right, if you two have finished playing, we have some things to talk about," Oma says, brushing the rubber spider away. "I'm going to apply for a job. And

I think you should look for one too, Peter. School starts soon, but maybe you could do some part-time work. Or you could start collecting for the recycling centers again with your friend Hubert. He dropped by earlier and said this was yours . . . Thank you, Peter. Every little bit helps."

Oma is holding Hubert's money.

—

"*Wie geht's?*" Peter greets Otto as he steps out onto the rooftop. "How's it going?"

Otto looks up. "What happened to you?" he asks, pointing at Peter's face.

"Thanks for reminding me," says Peter, touching his bruised face and wincing. "Nothing. I don't want to talk about it."

Otto is on his knees in front of a collection of building materials. The pigeons are circling above.

"Wow! Where did you get all that?" Peter asks.

"Let's just say I have my connections," says Otto, sharply focused on what he's doing.

Spread out around Otto are various lengths of sticks neatly lined up. There's a ball of wire, pliers, wire cutters, string, nails, screws, bolts, ropes and a collection of leather belts.

But what really grabs Peter's attention are a couple of books opened to illustrations and photographs of flying machines. Otto also has a notebook with scribbles and sketches of things that look like giant kites. Did he draw those? Peter wonders, impressed.

"Obviously I don't have everything at this stage. The most important thing we still need to get is the material to make the wings, or, in this case, one giant wing." Otto flicks a page in his book. "Between the two of us we should be able to find some sort of fabric that will be big enough to spread over the frame I'm going to build. Something that is light but strong enough to catch the wind without tearing."

Peter's a little baffled by Otto's sudden enthusiasm, but he's also getting very excited.

"What sort of sticks are they?" he asks. "And what's with the books?"

"They're bamboo. And the books I've had since I was your age – they're all about the history of flying. Like this one. It's about Otto Lilienthal, one of the great pioneers of aviation – and he was German. He was the first person to make a successful flight with a glider, about eighty years ago, actually not too far from here."

"Wow!" Peter says. "And he was called Otto too?"

"All the great people are." Otto grins. "And this

other book is all about Leonardo da Vinci."

"The famous Italian artist?" Peter asks. He remembers learning about him at school.

"He was more than just an artist," Otto adds. "He was a scientist, an inventor, a mathematician, a genius! And he was fascinated by flying. Here, look at these. They're drawings of how he thought people could fly. This crazy contraption is called an ornithopter."

On the page is a drawing of what looks like the skeleton of a bird with material stretched over the bones of the wings. It looks as though it's designed to be attached to a person's body.

"Amazing," Peter says. "So my idea about flying is starting to look good now, huh?"

"Your plan was to collect feathers, glue them together and fall to your death," Otto snorts. "Not good. My plan is to make a glider that has real aviation science behind it and that actually might work for us."

"For us?" Peter says.

"You, me, whoever!" says Otto. "Don't think for one second this isn't still a crazy and dangerous idea, but sometimes it's the crazy and dangerous ideas that give us the most hope, right?"

Peter notices a small duffel bag filled with tools

beside Otto.

"What kind work do you do?" Peter asks.

"I'm an apprentice carpenter, but right now I've been conscripted to carry and lay bricks. Look, Peter, if this is going to work we have got to get a move on. Time is against us. I've heard that the government is planning to put barbed wire on the rooftops. They're even planning to demolish entire buildings."

"How do you know all this?"

"I heard it on the construction site."

"Construction site?" Peter repeats. "What are you building?"

"What d'ya think?" says Otto. "*Die Mauer* – the Wall."

Der Pfeil
THE ARROW

When it's time to go and wave to his parents, Peter leaves Otto still working. On his way down the stairwell he spots Elke standing at the door of an apartment. He steps back and hides behind a column.

Elke hasn't seen him. She's talking to someone in the doorway. She pulls two halves of a broken arrow from inside her shirt.

"Look, Mama! I broke it. It snapped in two when it hit the target. Must've been faulty to begin with. I've only got one left," she says. "I'm getting so much better, though. Papa will be proud of me."

"Shhh! Come inside," Elke's mother says, pulling her in and closing the door behind them.

An arrow? Peter wonders as he hurries down the stairwell and steps out onto the street. Who has arrows? Maybe she's in an archery club. It can't be an escape plan – what kind of *verrückt*, crazy, escape would involve an arrow?

On his way to Invalidenstrasse, Peter is almost knocked over by a group of university students charging past him. They're running in the direction of the nearest border checkpoint.

"What's going on?" Peter calls out after them.

No one answers him, so he gives chase until he catches up with them.

"What's going on?" Peter asks again, running in step with one of the students. "Has someone escaped?"

"No! The opposite!" pants the student. "Someone tried to climb over and was shot. And he's been left to bleed to death on the barbed wire."

Peter slows to a stop and watches the students run off into the distance. He wants to know if it's true, but he doesn't really want to see it. Knowing for sure that someone has been killed for trying to escape unnerves him. He slowly turns and heads back toward Invalidenstrasse.

When Peter reaches the checkpoint, he sees that the border police have cordoned off a larger zone around the barbed-wire barrier. Peter is now standing farther back from where he stood the last time, but he can still see people over in the West. He scans the crowd and spots his father standing on the base of a lamppost waving frantically.

Peter's heart races. Good idea! he thinks, taking his father's lead and climbing onto the base of a nearby lamppost. He waves back.

Then Peter's father jumps down and his mother appears in his place. Peter catches his breath. He waves to her and she blows kisses back in his direction. They hold up Margrit, who waves and yells something he can't hear.

"I've got to get over there." Peter sighs, feeling more determined than ever.

"*Herunterkommen!* Get down from there!" one of the guards orders, marching up to the lamppost.

Peter does as he's told.

"Move on!" the guard demands.

"But my parents are over there," Peter says. "I just want to see them."

"I don't care," the guard says coldly. "*Hau ab!* Get moving!"

Peter cranes his neck to catch a glimpse of his parents one last time before he turns away.

Walking home he takes a detour through Elke's

neighborhood to look out for the pigeons. He spots Elke disappearing through the front archway of an abandoned building.

The city is dotted with buildings like these, damaged by shooting and bombs during the war and never repaired. Waiting to be demolished, they're just part of the drab landscape.

What's she up to now? he thinks. He crosses the street and walks through the archway that leads into the courtyard in the middle of the big square building. There's rubbish and junk everywhere. Peter tiptoes around the garbage, trying not to make a sound. He freezes when a rat crosses his path.

When Peter steps out into the courtyard, he sees Elke. She has her back to him. The ground is completely overgrown with weeds and grass and the high walls of the abandoned building loom on all four sides.

He steps back into the shadows and watches Elke. She's holding a bow and eyeing a large square plank of wood propped up against the wall on the other side of the courtyard. It's covered with chalk-drawn circles and a bull's-eye.

Peter watches as Elke positions her body, her feet shoulder-width apart. She points the bow toward the ground and attaches the back of the arrow to the center of the bowstring. She holds the arrow on the string with three fingers, raises the bow, pulls back on the string and points the arrow at the plank of wood.

After a second, she releases her grip and in a flash the arrow shoots across the courtyard and hits the target with a loud *thump*.

Elke has hit a bull's-eye!

She looks pretty pleased with herself as she punches her fist above her head.

Peter hears some boys outside on the street shouting to each other. Oma and Opa are probably wondering where I am, he thinks. He leaves Elke to her bow and arrow.

Before going home, though, Peter makes one more stop – at Hubert's place. He's not sure whether to tell him off for giving Oma the money or thank him.

When the Ackermanns' apartment door swings open, Hubert's mother is standing there. She looks distressed.

"Oh, it's you, Peter." Wiping away her tears, Frau Ackermann steps aside and ushers Peter into the hall. "I thought it was the police. Hubert!"

Hubert runs from his room and hugs Peter tightly. He's crying and can hardly speak.

Peter is stunned. He's never seen his friend crying

before. "What's going on?"

"It's Ralf," Hubert sobs. "He's dead. They shot him trying to escape over the barrier."

Schmerzen
PAIN

Peter is playing with the food on his plate. He doesn't feel like eating. No one he knows has died before. Seeing Hubert and his mother in such pain has made him miss his family even more.

"Hubert's poor mother," says Oma, taking Opa's plate from the table. "I told you they mean business."

Opa grunts. Peter looks at him. His brow is furrowed. He appears angry and upset.

"Again . . ." he begins to slur. "Never learn," he manages to say.

"Oh, Ernst, *mein Schatz*," says Oma, sitting next to him and holding his hand, comforting him. "Peter, go get some coal. I'll heat up some water for Opa's bath."

Peter grabs the tin buckets from under the sink. He walks the five floors down to the basement and fills the buckets with coal. His arms strain as he slowly carries them back up the stairs.

They're lucky. Most apartments in his building don't have a toilet, but at least there's one on every floor for the residents. As for their bathtub, well, "That's a luxury!" Oma always says.

Once back in the apartment Peter shovels coal into the bottom of the stove, and Oma places a large pot of water on one of the hot plates. When the water is heated, Oma and Peter carefully carry the pot and pour it into the bathtub.

"All right, you help Opa undress," Oma instructs. She runs her fingers through the water. "That's warm enough. Slowly now."

Oma leaves the room, and Peter takes his opa's left arm, placing it around his neck, and puts his arm around Opa's waist.

"That's it, Opa," Peter says, lifting Opa's motionless right leg. He lowers it into the tub. Opa sits on the edge of the bath and hoists his left leg in. He slides into the water, exhaling deeply.

"*Schön warm, nicht wahr?* Nice and warm, huh?" says Peter, sponging water onto his opa's shoulders.

Peter is considering telling Opa about his plan, but

he's distracted by the crosshatch of deep scars across his grandfather's back. He has never thought much about them before – they're just a part of Opa – but now he realizes they must have been from his time in the Soviet camp.

"Opa, what did they do to you?" Peter asks. He reaches out to touch Opa's back.

Opa pulls away and frowns.

"I'm sorry," Peter says, quickly dunking the sponge back into the bathwater.

Opa seems upset, as if he had forgotten they were there and Peter has reminded him. But after a few minutes he turns his face to Peter.

"Punish . . . ment," he slurs. "For trying . . . to escape."

Peter feels his stomach tied up in knots.

"*Nicht flüchten!* No escaping . . . Ralf . . ." Peter sees tears come to his opa's eyes. "Not you," he says. "Not you."

Peter sighs. "No, Opa, not me."

—

Later that night, Peter lies motionless in his bed staring at the ceiling. He can't stop thinking of Ralf and wondering what he felt, slumped over the wire and left to die. He had everyone here, but he was still prepared to risk his own life for freedom.

I have Opa and Oma. Am I really going to risk my life?

Peter searches for an answer, but his head sinks deeper into his pillow and he dozes off . . .

Flying.

Birdlike.

Feathered arms.

Flapping.

Overjoyed.

Over buildings.

Over the Wall.

Goodbye, East.

Hello, West.

He soars.

He glides.

And below.

Looking up.

His family.

His father.

His sister.

His mother.

"Peter!" she calls.

But then . . .

Guns fire.

Bullets whiz.

They hit.

They sting.

They pierce Peter's wings.

And he begins to fall.

And fall.

And fall.

"Peter!" screams his mother.

"Peter!"

Peter jolts up out of his sleep. He hears Oma crying out to him. "Peter! Peter! Peter!" And his opa's slurred attempts to call his name.

He springs out of bed and runs to his grandparents' bedroom.

Oma is on the floor clasping her back. Opa is moaning, struggling to get out of bed – desperately trying to get to her.

"It's my back," Oma groans. "I was helping your opa to roll over. *Bitte*, Peter, get me a hot-water bottle. The coals should still be warm enough to boil some water."

Peter carefully helps Oma up and back into bed. She grimaces in pain. He finds the oval-shaped metal bottle and fills it with hot water. He gently places it against Oma's lower back.

She sighs with relief.

Peter wonders what they would do without him. Who would be here to help if he'd gone with his parents to the West that day? Who will be here to help, when he escapes?

Die Zeit Vergeht
RUNNING OUT OF TIME

Peter leaves early. He writes a note saying he's going to collect bottles for the recycling center and puts it on the kitchen table for Oma to find.

As he leaves, he looks for the two men in a car parked outside his building, the ones that Frau Roeder told Oma about. But they are nowhere to be seen, and the street looks deserted.

Outside Hubert's building Peter spots a policeman. He's talking to a mother pushing a stroller – and making silly expressions at the baby who's giggling.

The officer is a tall skinny man with enormous bushy eyebrows, even bushier than Opa's. They're so big that Peter finds it difficult to look anywhere else –

they look like two dancing, hairy caterpillars.

"What are you staring at?" the policeman says.

"Nothing, but you have the perfect face to make babies laugh," says Peter. He quickly edges around the officer and the mother and stroller.

"Wise guy, eh? You're just lucky I'm in a good mood this morning, boy," says Officer Eyebrows. "Otherwise I'd lock you up for disrespecting an official of the state. Now scram!"

Peter runs off and doesn't stop until he reaches Elke's building. On the rooftop he says hello to the pigeons toddling about in the coop. Peter reaches in and gently picks up Felix – his favorite. He cradles him and pats him softly. Felix coos loudly and nudges his small head against Peter's thumb.

"They're happy to see you. Especially Felix."

Peter jumps in surprise. Otto is standing at the edge of the roof looking out over the Wall.

"I didn't see you there! You're not working today?" Peter asks, noticing some new materials on the roof. "What's with the two large planks of wood? And the canvas sheet? And the pots of plants?"

"I'm working later," Otto says. "If we're going to build a glider right here in the open, we'll need a place to hide it. So I'm going to build a garden bed . . . well, make it look as if I'm building a garden bed. We'll hide the construction of the glider under the canvas and place the two wooden planks and plants on top. People believe everything they read, so we'll put up a sign saying *Garden Under Construction* or something like that."

"Well, you've really thought this through." Peter grins, once again impressed.

"We have to be more careful," Otto says, taking Felix from Peter and placing him back in the coop with the other pigeons. "Did you hear about the student yesterday? Shot dead and left to die on the barbed wire."

Peter sighs heavily. "I know him. I mean, I knew him."

"Really? I'm sorry," says Otto, turning his back on Peter and looking out over the city again. He doesn't say anything else and the silence feels awkward.

"Um, Otto?" Peter says. "You okay?"

Otto spins round. "Look, Peter, this might be getting too dangerous. Perhaps we should reconsider," he says. "I figure we have a couple of days at most before this whole area is totally secured. And to be honest, I don't know if it will work. We don't even have the right material to stretch over the glider frame –"

"No!" Peter cuts Otto off. "No! Don't say that. It can

work. It has to work. You said so yourself. You drew out plans and everything. Plus this garden bed cover-up is just brilliant. And, well, just tell me what sort of material we need and I'll find it. What about that canvas or a bedsheet?"

"Cotton's heavy and rips too easily. Otto Lilienthal did use cotton linen for his flights. But he had a long launchpad, running down hills for takeoff. With only fifteen meters to run before the jump, we need a fabric that's light but strong enough to capture the airstream underneath it. Maybe silk."

"Silk? Where are we going to get silk?" Peter asks.

Otto sighs again and shrugs.

But Peter is determined not to give up.

—

Peter's mind races as he steps out onto the street. As he's about to set off, a boy on a bike rides past. It's Max.

Peter looks down and marches along quickly, hoping Max doesn't spot him.

But he does. At least he appears to be alone this time. He circles back to ride just behind Peter. "What are you up to? Who do you know who lives in this neighborhood, rat?"

"Leave me alone, Max," Peter says. "We used to be friends, but now you're treating me as if I'm the enemy."

Max just sneers. "You *are* the enemy."

"*Wirklich?* Really, Max? We've known each other since we were little. This is crazy!"

"I heard about Hubert's brother," Max says. "That's what you deserve when you're a traitor. I thought Hubert was my friend, but his family were always against the government. I'm glad they caught Ralf. All deserters should be shot."

Peter stops dead in his tracks. Max has to slam on his brakes so that he doesn't run into him. Peter gives Max the dirtiest of looks and for a moment Max appears petrified. He knows he's gone too far.

Peter stares at him in disgust. "Do you seriously believe that?" he asks, coldly. "Do you really think another human being should die for wanting a better life?"

The question throws Max off. He stutters to find the right comeback.

Peter shakes his head and walks on. "You really are a *Schwachkopf*," he says. "A total blockhead!"

Max doesn't follow, but he shouts out after him. "I know you're up to something."

Peter pretends he hasn't heard. He won't give Max

the satisfaction of seeing how that has rattled him. With Max snooping around and the Wall getting stronger, Peter knows time really is running out.

Goldene Zwanziger
THE GOLDEN TWENTIES

Peter loiters around the Invalidenstrasse checkpoint hoping to see his family over in the West. But the barbed wire has been replaced with large concrete blocks. It's now almost impossible to see anyone.

When he turns onto the street where he spotted Elke practicing her archery skills, he decides to revisit the abandoned building to see if she's there.

She isn't. So when Peter steps into the courtyard he makes his way over to the target board.

She's really good, he thinks, impressed by the dents directly around the bull's-eye. But why? Who even does this?

Peter takes a closer look at the target. He pulls

it toward him and spots something behind it. It's Elke's bow and arrow.

She could've found a better hiding place, he thinks, picking them up.

Peter walks back across the courtyard.

How hard can it be? He raises the bow, fumbling as he tries to hook the back of the arrow, the nock, into the string. Peter has never done this before. He raises the bow and points in the direction of the target and pulls back on the string. His arm wobbles a little as he tries to keep the shaft of the arrow steady. He grits his teeth and counts under his breath.

"*Eins . . . zwei . . . drei –*"

"What do you think you're doing?" A voice echoes across the courtyard just as he releases the arrow.

It's Elke.

The arrow whooshes way over the target board – and flies through one of the broken windows of the abandoned building.

"No!" Elke cries, racing over to Peter. "Didn't anyone ever tell you not to touch things that don't belong to you?" She sighs, looking frustrated. "Come on!"

"Where?" Peter asks, following her.

"Arrows are hard to come by. And very expensive.

You have to help me get it back."

Peter follows her to the main entrance of the building on the opposite side of the courtyard. The doors are locked and many of the windows are covered with boards.

Elke climbs up a pile of rubble.

"Have you been in here before?" asks Peter.

"No. I just use the courtyard," says Elke. She grabs a rock and drags an empty bottle crate over to another window. Climbing onto it, she breaks what seems like the only uncracked windowpane. "By the way, how did you find it? Are you spying on me?"

"No! Um, yes, um, sort of . . . sorry," Peter stutters. "You're not actually going in there, are you?"

"You're right. I should make you go in alone and retrieve it."

Peter shakes his head.

"Yeah, that's what I thought," she says. She begins to climb through the window, carefully avoiding the broken glass around the edges.

"What are you doing with a bow and arrow anyway?" Peter asks, scrambling up behind her.

Elke doesn't answer Peter as she slides down a pile of rubbish inside. Peter follows, loses his footing, and bumps into her.

"Hey! *Pass auf!* Watch it!" snaps Elke.

"Whew! It stinks in here. Like old shoes and mouse poop." It takes Peter a couple of minutes for his eyes to adjust to the dim light, but when he looks up he's amazed.

They're surrounded by ornate wooden paneling, high ceilings and a rusty wrought iron curved staircase with elaborate curls and swirl patterns on the railing. He's never seen anything like this room. "Wow, what was this place?"

"Who knows?" Elke says, trampling through the rubbish and advancing farther into the cavernous room. "It's a shame all these beautiful buildings have been left to rot since the war."

Peter reaches up to open the heavy drapes from one of the windows. But with a *crack* and then a loud whooshing and crashing sound, they detach from the wall and fall to the ground.

Peter is left standing by the window, covered in dust and coughing.

"What are you doing?" Elke cries, bounding over to Peter. "Are you all right?"

"Yes," Peter splutters, brushing the dust and grime off himself. "I just wanted to get some light in here – so we can see what we're doing."

Elke gasps. "Look!"

Peter turns to see that the high walls are lined with mirrors from floor to ceiling. On the other side of the room is a stage framed with murals of partygoers in old-fashioned clothes, drinking and dancing.

"Was this some kind of theater?" Peter asks, still coughing.

"It must have been an old music hall, a cabaret theater," Elke says excitedly. She climbs up a set of steps that lead onto the stage. "Look at me! I'm an actress!"

Peter grins. He joins her on stage.

"This is incredible," Elke adds. "This must be from the Golden Twenties!"

"The what?" asks Peter.

"Come on, you don't even know your own city's history? It was before the war, when this city was famous for art, music, fashion, film, books and dancing. Everyone in the world wanted to come here."

"How do you know all this?" Peter asks.

"When my oma was alive she used to tell me stories about when she was young."

Peter wonders if his oma and opa ever visited this theater, ever laughed and danced here together. But then something catches his eye. He walks over to the stage to take a closer look at the stage curtains, which hang from the very high ceiling and drape all the way down to the floor.

"Are you planning to pull those curtains down too?" Elke jokes. "What are you doing?"

"What's this material?" Peter asks, rubbing the bright-yellow lining of the heavy curtain.

Elke joins him and strokes the smooth, shiny fabric. "It's silk," she says.

Tanzen
DANCING

Peter can't believe his luck.

"Silk? Are you sure?" he asks. Silk was exactly the thing Otto was looking for – the perfect material for making a durable wing for the glider.

"Yes, I'm sure," Elke says. "What's going on? Why are you so excited about this? Do you and your oma make dresses for extra money?"

"No!" Peter snorts, sizing up the curtain.

He calculates that the silk lining is about seven meters by twelve meters – more than enough to form the glider's wing.

"Has this got something to do with you trying to get to the West?" Elke asks.

"Of course not," Peter says, a little too quickly. "What about your bow and arrow? Has that got something to do with you trying to get to the West?"

"Of course not," Elke says, also a little too quickly.

They exchange looks and then laugh in unison.

"You're not going to tell me, are you?" Elke says, smirking.

"Well, *you're* not going to tell me, are you?" Peter says.

Elke sighs. "I can't."

"I can't either."

"Then we'll just go about doing our own thing, I guess. But right now I'm going to look for my arrow." Elke steps back to the middle of the stage. She does a twirl, as if a spotlight is shining on her and sings, "La-la-la!"

Peter smiles at her and then looks up at the curtains. They'll be harder to pull down than the window curtains, he thinks. He wonders what his next move should be.

I'll have to come back with a knife and cut out a large enough panel of the lining, or perhaps I'll just take the whole thing, he thinks. Fold it up, maybe. But how am I going to carry such a large piece of bright-yellow material to Otto's rooftop without drawing attention?

"Peter! Come over here!" Elke calls.

Peter joins Elke at the center of the stage. She reaches out her hands toward him.

"What?" Peter asks, stepping back. "What are you doing?"

"Dance with me!"

"Huh?"

"Just do it. Don't be a baby," Elke orders, grabbing Peter's right hand and putting it on her hip, and clasping his left hand with her right hand. "Now move with me from side to side."

"But there's no music and what about your arrow and –"

"Relax." Elke smiles as she waltzes around the stage with Peter. "That's it. Just step and glide . . . it's easy."

Peter has never danced like this with a girl before. Actually, he can't even remember the last time he danced. Maybe when he was little. It feels strange, but nice strange. He begins to mirror Elke's smile and relaxes a bit.

"Now you're getting it," she says. "Imagine dancing back here when this place was built. Imagine feeling light and happy and never worrying about what was going to happen next."

Peter looks out at the big room and imagines it

filled with people dancing to a band playing on the stage. He's surprised by how nice it feels to be holding Elke's hand.

"Do you think you'll ever see your mother and father again?" she asks.

"Yes," Peter says, determined to believe that he will, even though there's a part of him that is deeply afraid that he won't. "Do you think you'll see your father again?"

"Yes," says Elke, sounding just as determined. "I have to see him. I miss him. My mother says we're the same, like peas in a pod."

"Did he teach you how to use the bow and arrow?" Peter asks.

Elke pauses and looks Peter in the eye before she answers. Her stare is intense but honest. Peter smiles nervously. She smiles back.

"Yes," she says. "He taught me. He was a champion archer. So . . . what about you? Are you closer to your mother or to your father?"

"Um, probably my mother. Although I know I annoy her when I don't do as I'm told – which is probably most of the time. My father is away for work a lot. He works long hours at a cinema on the Kurfürstendamm and he's always tired, so we never really talk that much. And I'm close to my little sister

– I really miss her. And then there's Opa and Oma, and well –"

Before Peter can finish his sentence Elke leans in and kisses him on the cheek. It catches him off guard, and he can feel his face heating up like the coals in Oma's stove.

He gulps. "Wha . . . wha . . . what was that for?"

"Just because," she says.

Peter looks away, hoping that she can't see how red his face is. He spots Elke's arrow on the floor below the stage. "Hey, there it is!" he cries, breaking apart from her.

He jumps off the stage, scoops it up and hands it back up to Elke.

"Well, I better get going," he says, feeling awkward.

"Okay, I'm going to practice some more," says Elke, inspecting the arrow for damage. "See you around."

"Yeah, um, *bis bald*, Elke!" says Peter as he runs for the window.

—

The following morning, Peter is wearing his best clothes – wool slacks, an ironed shirt and tie. The collar of his shirt is stiffer and tighter around his neck than the usual shirts he wears and his pants are made of an itchy material that clings to the back of his calves.

He's not looking forward to the day. He's never been to a funeral before. It's going to be horribly sad and he doesn't know what he'll say to Hubert. He still can't believe that Ralf is gone. Hubert hasn't come out of his room since hearing the news.

"You could at least have combed your hair," says Oma, wetting her hand at the sink and patting his hair down. "It's sticking up all over the place."

"Bye, Opa," Peter says. Opa is sitting at the table reading a newspaper. The paper shakes as he turns the page. Oma kisses him on the forehead.

"We'll only be gone for a couple of hours, *mein Schatz*," she says. "I have some food here for you, and water – all very easy to reach."

Opa nods. "*Macht jetzt end . . . lich los!*" he slurs. "Get going."

—

When they reach the church, Peter is surprised to see such a large crowd milling outside. So many people have come to pay their respects to Ralf.

There are even reporters hovering about, taking photos of Hubert and his family as they enter the church. Most people seem wary of having their picture taken, probably because they're attending the funeral of someone who has tried to escape. Many of the mourners turn the other way when a camera is pointed toward them.

Peter finally spots Hubert. Hubert doesn't see him, though. His mother is holding him close and his head is buried deep in her embrace. Seeing this makes Peter miss his own mother even more.

Oma and Peter join the stream of people entering the church. Oma makes her way up to the front pews. Peter wishes they could sit at the back.

The service begins and the minister starts by making some remarks about Ralf's young life and how it was cut so short.

Peter eyes are fixed on the coffin. He's never even thought about death before. Dying is for old people, he thinks. Not for young people. Not for people like Ralf.

He looks at Oma and sees a tear running down her cheek. He glances across the aisle and sees Hubert looking back at him. Peter nods at him. He nods back, his eyes red and teary.

Peter's mouth is dry. He feels a lump in his throat. Taking Oma's hand, he squeezes it tightly. She seems surprised and leans in to kiss him on the top of his head. Peter's mind flashes back to when he was a little boy and Oma would hold him tightly in her arms whenever he was tired or upset and quietly sing old folk songs to him.

He realizes how much he'll miss her when he escapes to the West.

After the service Oma and Peter make their way over to Hubert's family. Oma manages to push her way past the relatives and friends around them. She offers her condolences to Hubert's mother and father.

"Thank you," Frau Ackermann says softly, looking down at Peter and gently touching his cheek where it is still swollen from the fight. "Your grandson is such a good friend to Hubert."

Hubert steps up to Peter and hugs him. "I'm glad you're here, Peter," he says, adjusting his spectacles. "You're a true friend. You know what it's like to be trapped here. From now on I'm not going to be afraid to speak the truth. From now on I'll be more like my brother."

Peter notices people are looking in their direction. They can hear what Hubert is saying and they look a little nervous.

"Are you all right?" Peter asks.

"No, not really. None of us are – we're all trapped on this side of the Wall."

"Hubert!" his mother snaps. "Please, this is not the time."

"I'm speaking up for Ralf, Mutti! I'm his voice now!"

Hubert's mother hurries to his side, tugs at his sleeve and shushes him. "You could get us all in trouble," she whispers. "There are eyes watching us."

Peter looks up and understands what Frau Ackermann means. He notices two men in the crowd who he's never seen before. They are wearing almost identical suits and look sort of official. Peter wonders if these might be the two men Frau Roeder was talking about.

"I don't care who's listening," Hubert says loudly. "My brother is a hero!"

Everyone turns. Frau Ackermann cups her hand over Hubert's mouth. She's very upset.

"*Bitte*, Hubert! Don't do this. Not now," she pleads, pulling Hubert into her and hugging him tightly. "You go with Peter now," she says. "While I talk to the others, but, *bitte* . . . no more of that talk."

Hubert and Peter step away from the adults.

"He is, you know – a hero." Hubert sniffs, wiping away his tears with the back of his hand.

Peter nods and flops his arm over Hubert's

shoulder. He has an idea that might help him and cheer Hubert up too.

"I'm sorry this has happened," Peter says, "but I've got a brilliant plan. Ralf would have liked it. Do you want to help?"

Hubert stops sniffing, and looks directly at Peter.

"A plan?" he says. "Has it got something to do with escaping?"

Peter looks over his shoulder to make sure no one is listening. He nods. "Yes. And I'm going to need your recycling cart."

Die Schubkarre
THE CART

"What is this place?" Hubert asks Peter, as they wheel the large recycling cart into the courtyard of the abandoned building.

The cart is a wagon-like one – a large wooden box secured on a flat base and four wheels, with a long metal handle attached at the front to pull it along. It's stacked with piles of newspapers.

"You'll see," says Peter, pulling the cart toward the window through which he and Elke had entered the theater. "Right, follow me."

"In there?" says Hubert, following Peter, who is already climbing into the building. "Is it safe?"

Hubert is not as impressed by the grand room and

the giant mirrored wall as Peter and Elke were.

"It's creepy!" he says, keeping close to Peter. "I bet it's haunted. Definitely feels like it's haunted."

They step onto the stage. "I need to pull these curtains down somehow," Peter says, grabbing on to them.

"Huh? Are you going to tell me why?"

"Not just yet," Peter says. "But it's good. Trust me."

Peter pulls on the curtains as hard as he can, hoping they will collapse to the stage floor. They don't.

Hubert lets out a sharp whistle from behind him. Peter turns to see him at the back of the stage, winding a winch in a counterclockwise motion. He gestures to Peter to look up. The curtains are attached to a long bar at the top, and as Hubert winds the winch, both the bar and the curtains effortlessly lower to the floor and gather at Peter's feet.

"Now what?" Hubert smirks, swaggering back over to Peter.

Peter laughs. "Nice one! Can you help me cut out the lining?" Peter hands him a pair of scissors. "You start at that end and I'll start at this end. We have to make sure we cut it out in one whole piece."

Once the boys are finished cutting, Peter begins to fold the silk.

"Now all we have to do is make sure we're able to hide this under the newspapers on your recycling cart . . ." Peter says. He's so excited that he can hardly keep the feeling in.

"And then you're going to take it where? And what are you going to do with it? Come on, Peter, tell me!" Hubert presses.

Peter wants to tell him, but he doesn't know how much he should reveal. "I haven't stopped thinking about this since I woke up this morning – I'm worried that if I tell you my plan I'll get you into trouble. That's the last thing your family needs right now – they're already a target. At least if we get caught you can say you didn't know what I was doing."

"I don't care," Hubert says. "I don't care anymore what they do to me. Not the Stasi and not the NPA."

"But I care!" Peter retorts. "And it could put me in danger too . . ."

Hubert looks hurt. He begins walking away from Peter.

"Hey! Where are you going?" Peter calls after him. "Hubert, come back."

But Hubert doesn't. "If you don't trust me, then I'm leaving," he says.

"Well, can I still borrow the cart?" Peter adds, feeling like a terrible friend as he says it.

Hubert nods as he climbs out the window.

Peter jumps off the stage and runs to the window. He watches Hubert cross the courtyard, leaving the cart behind.

Once Peter folds up the curtain and wraps it in newspaper, he places it on the bottom of the cart and stacks the bundles of tied newspapers on top. The perfect hiding place, he thinks, wheeling the cart out of the courtyard and onto Gartenstrasse.

He heads in the direction of Otto's rooftop. But he doesn't get very far before he hears the whirl of bicycle wheels behind him. It's Max again.

"What were you doing in there?" he asks. "What is that place?"

Peter ignores him and keeps walking. Max grumbles, then turns around and heads back to the abandoned building. Peter hopes that Elke doesn't show up while he's snooping about.

At the next corner, Peter can see a police officer giving directions to an older man. As he gets closer he realizes it's Officer Eyebrows.

"You've got to be kidding," Peter says under his breath.

"Ah, it's you again, wise guy," the officer says, stepping in front of him. "At least you're working. I see you're off to the recycling center."

Peter nods. He steers the cart around Officer Eyebrows.

"Hey!" he snaps. "Watch the toes!" The officer pulls the cart back toward him and grabs a newspaper from the top of the pile. One of the ties comes loose, and the stacks shift a little to the side.

"You've got quite a few here," he says.

Peter tries his hardest to stay calm. If the policeman digs a little deeper, he's sure to find the fabric. It's obviously hidden, and Peter doesn't know how to explain it.

"Well, I better get going," he says.

"*Halt!*" Officer Eyebrows snaps. "Why is the bottom layer of papers hanging over the cart like that? Not a very good stacking job, if you ask me."

Peter feels his heart beating faster.

"I really must go," he says as politely as he can.

"Hold on! What's that yellow cloth?" the policeman says.

Peter can't believe it. A piece of the curtain has slipped out from its newspaper wrapping. Any moment now, he'll be caught. He frantically tries to think up a cover story.

But then Peter hears yelling coming from behind them, and it's getting closer . . .

Officer Eyebrows and Peter turn to see Hubert,

now on his bike, pedaling straight for them – and shouting like some sort of madman.

"Slow down!" Officer Eyebrows shouts at Hubert. "*Halt! Halt!*"

But Hubert doesn't slow down. He pedals faster. And screams some more. Peter dives out of the way. His friend whizzes by and reaches up to grab Officer Eyebrows' police hat off his head.

"Hey!" cries Officer Eyebrows, turning on his heels and sprinting after Hubert. "Come back with my hat!"

Peter can't believe it. Hubert just saved me, he thinks, grabbing his cart and hurrying off in the opposite direction.

He saved me. And the plan too!

Rasen
SPEEDING

"This is incredible!" Otto says. "Silk! And so much of it!"

Peter and Otto unfold the lining of the stage curtain and lay it out flat on the rooftop. Otto places a couple of potted plants on the corners of the giant fabric, so it won't be swept away by the wind.

Peter is still edgy as he tells Otto about Officer Eyebrows. But Otto laughs when he tells him about Hubert snatching the man's hat.

"You should have told him you were making flags for the Free German Youth," he says. "It's almost the same color as their flag."

"Do you think we have enough to make the perfect

gliding wing?" Peter asks.

"I think we have more than enough," Otto says. "Still doesn't mean it's going to work, though."

"When do you think I should do this? How long will it take you to construct it? Would it be quicker if I help you –"

"Hey! Slow down!" Otto cuts in. "Don't get too excited, but I think I should be able to make it in the next few hours." Otto gestures Peter over to the garden bed and he lifts up the canvas to reveal an A-frame. Otto has built the main section of the glider already.

It's amazing.

"Looks good, right?" Otto says. "Took a bit of effort to attach and wire all the bamboo together. So, let's say tomorrow morning, right at the crack of dawn – a little bit of daylight will help, but you don't want it to be too light."

Peter nods. His chest tightens and his stomach churns. He's excited and nervous at the same time. He can't believe his crazy plan is actually coming together.

—

After leaving the rooftop Peter walks toward the Invalidenstrasse checkpoint. Seeing Mutti, Vati and Margrit wave to me today would be perfect, he thinks, if I'm going to escape tomorrow.

Peter can't believe how fast the Wall is going up. The narrow view he had over into the West, only a couple of days ago, is now entirely blocked. There are even more military personnel and vehicles in the area. Peter sighs. He isn't going to see his family today.

Oh, well, by this time tomorrow I'll be with them anyway, and we'll be able to have a party to celebrate my escape, he thinks. Peter grins and decides to head back home. When he crosses the street he sees Elke striding at a clipped pace, her fiery red hair tied back.

What's she up to now? he wonders as she darts down an alley parallel with the Wall.

Peter follows her, doing his best not to lose her but staying at a safe distance so she doesn't spot him.

Elke turns left into another narrow street that heads back in the direction of the Wall. Peter peeks around the corner. It looks as if she's heading to an unguarded section of the Wall. It's high and old – it was clearly there long before the barrier went up.

She stands right up against the Wall and, strangely, it looks as if she's talking into it. Elke bends down and puts her hand through what looks like a small hole in the barrier. It soon dawns on Peter that she's talking to someone on the other side.

After about ten minutes, Elke strides back in Peter's direction. He ducks behind a couple of parked Trabants, but at that moment Peter becomes aware of a rumbling sound echoing from way down at the other end of the street. He turns to see what it is and his jaw drops. An army tank is thundering over the cobblestones, heading directly toward the Wall – and Elke!

Oh, no! Peter thinks.

"ELKE!" he shouts just as the tank thunders past him. "Get out of the way!"

He's lost sight of her. His view is blocked by the armored vehicle. And the tank is accelerating.

Peter bolts after it. "ELKE!" he hollers again. Has she gotten out of the way in time?

The tank engine roars and revs louder as it careens toward the Wall.

"Peter!" Elke cries as she lunges out from a recessed doorway and smacks right into him.

They embrace and turn to see the tank smashing into the Wall.

KAAAAABOOOOM!

The impact is deafening as concrete blocks shatter. The tank is now wedged in the rubble, and within a minute police sirens are howling from the surrounding streets.

The hatch on the tank flips open. A young man crawls out, scrambles over the vehicle, and leaps over into the West. Gunshots ring out. Soldiers running past Elke and Peter are firing their guns at the young man – only to have their shots met by bullets from the western side.

"Get down!" Peter yells, realizing they could easily be caught in the crossfire. But Elke is already dragging him to safety into the doorway.

Aufstehen!
GET UP!

Peter and Elke are crouched low in the doorway. They're petrified and decide to stay low, since the soldiers are still shouting and gunshots are still cracking across the streets.

"Are you all right?" gulps Elke, panting.

"I think so," Peter says, breathless, his cheek pressed against the door, only centimeters away from Elke's face. "Do you think he got away?"

"I hope so."

"Me too."

"Hey! *Ihr zwei – aufstehen!* You two – get up! And get out of here," a soldier orders, standing over Elke and Peter. "Now!"

Peter and Elke spring to their feet and bolt. Peter is too afraid to look back to see whether the young man who drove the tank has been able to escape the bullets. He's frightened about what he will see. Instead he runs as fast as he can with Elke at his side.

When they make it back to Peter's neighborhood, the two slow to a jog, then stop, gasping and holding each other up.

"I can't believe it," Elke says.

"Me neither," pants Peter. "What an unbelievable idea. Talk about a great escape plan – steal a tank and crash through the barrier! Why didn't I think of that?"

"Because where would you get a tank, *Dummkopf*?" says Elke, laughing. "They don't exactly park them in the street and leave the keys in."

Peter laughs. "True."

Elke narrows her eyes at him. "Were you spying on me again?" she asks.

"Not really. Sort of. Okay, yes. But not intentionally, I just followed you because I was curious," Peter says. "Who were you talking to? Through the Wall?"

Elke exhales. "My father. Everyone's been busy trying to wave to each other over the barrier, but we knew this wall had a hole in it. When the barbed wire was rolled out, my mother and I ran to this spot immediately – and so did my father."

"I wish my parents knew about that hole," Peter sighs. "Then we might have been able to talk today, which would have made all the difference."

"Why? What's so special about today?"

Peter is desperate to tell Elke that today is his last day in the East. He wishes he could say a proper goodbye. But he doesn't. He hesitates and instead musters up the courage to ask her something else.

"Elke, my oma said that she's going to make a treat tonight to have with dinner. She said with all the trouble around us we need something to raise our spirits. I'm guessing she's going to make my favorite dessert. Anyway . . . um, you could, um, come around if you like?"

Elke doesn't respond right away. It makes Peter regret that he asked. And his voice cracks when he adds, "But don't feel you have to. I mean, you know –"

"I would love to," says Elke. "But I have to ask my mother first."

"Oh, sure! Yes," says Peter. "Well, if you can, any time after seven. You know where I live, apartment five zero six. And –" He hesitates.

Elke nods. "And . . ."

Perhaps because he knows he might never see her again, or because he hasn't stopped thinking about dancing with her, or simply because he just feels great when he's with her, Peter leans forward and kisses Elke on the cheek.

"What was that for?" she asks.

"Just because," Peter says.

"Well, that's a good enough reason." Elke grins, then turns and runs off.

Peter's heart is pounding harder than when he saw the tank bust through the Wall.

—

Peter and Opa sit patiently at the kitchen table. Oma opens the refrigerator, and Peter hopes she's going to take out his favorite dessert. As she does, there's a knock at the door. Peter opens it and is surprised to see Hubert standing there.

"Ah, good timing," Oma says. "I asked Frau Ackermann if she would let Hubert drop by for some of this. Ta-da!"

Oma takes a tray out of the freezer compartment of the refrigerator and pops it on the table.

"Yes!" Peter say excitedly. "I knew it! My favorite – Kalter Hund cake!"

It's been a long time since Oma has made sweets, and the cake is incredible: it's chocolate, powdered sugar, milk and eggs all mixed together, poured over cookies and frozen. Peter's always loved this icy treat and its funny name – cold dog cake.

Peter grabs a knife and begins to cut it.

"Cold dog for everyone!" he says, and then a huge wave of wistfulness washes over him. This will be the last time we'll be eating together, he thinks.

"Thanks for today," Peter whispers to Hubert as Oma goes to get plates and forks. "Swiping the officer's hat was genius. Obviously he didn't catch you."

"There was no way he could catch me with those eyebrows weighing him down," Hubert snorts. "You're welcome, even if you won't tell me your plan. That's not going to stop me from helping you."

Peter knows how lucky he is to have such a loyal friend. He knows he has to tell him. "Tonight will be my last night in the East," he whispers.

"Escape?" Hubert mouths.

Peter nods.

"What are you two mumbling about?" says Oma, placing the plates on the table.

"Nothing," Peter says, hurriedly cutting into the cake.

They all eat in silence. The cake is too tasty to ruin with small talk.

When everyone is done eating, Hubert excuses himself and says he wants to get back home. Peter understands. It must feel strange for his friend to be enjoying himself and eating cake when he knows he'll never see his brother again. And he can't even imagine what it would be like if Hubert was the one escaping and he was staying behind.

"Good luck, Peter," Hubert whispers, hugging him tightly. "I'm proud of you and I know Ralf would've been too! Be safe."

Peter's stomach churns. He can't actually believe that he might not see his best friend again.

As he returns to the kitchen, another knock echoes through the apartment. Has Hubert come back to tell me not to go? he wonders.

Peter opens the door again, but it's Elke – smiling from ear to ear.

Warum?
WHY?

Opa keeps winking at Peter as he introduces Elke to Oma. Peter makes a face at him. He really wishes Opa would stop.

"And this is my opa," says Peter.

"A pleasure to meet you, sir," says Elke politely.

Peter shoots Opa a stern look.

"Would you like some Kalter Hund, dear?" says Oma, grabbing a clean plate.

Elke nods.

"Good. Sit down and make yourself comfortable."

After Oma serves the cake to Elke, she helps Opa up. "We'll leave you two alone to chat," she says.

Peter stands to help.

"We're all right," Oma says, as she and Opa shuffle out of the kitchen.

"Sorry about my opa," he says to Elke. "I'm glad that you were allowed to come."

"Oh, I wasn't allowed," says Elke. "Are you kidding? What mother would let their daughter go to a boy's house – a boy they've never met? No, I told her I was going to my friend Margot's place on the first floor of our building."

"But she lets you play with a bow and arrow in an abandoned building," Peter says.

"That's different," says Elke. "Anyway . . . I think your grandparents are very sweet. You're all sweet together. They must be relieved that you're not in the West with your parents and sister."

"Huh?" says Peter. "Relieved? What do you mean?"

"Well, they're old and they must feel safer knowing that they have you to look out for them. Who would be here to help take care of your opa? And they must miss your parents and your sister like crazy. Imagine if you were gone too."

"Um, yeah, I guess," Peter mumbles, not sure how he feels about that. He realizes he hasn't given enough thought to what his grandparents have been thinking or feeling since the Wall went up. Or what will happen after he leaves.

Peter shakes his head. But Elke presses on.

"Whatever your plan is, I'm sure they won't want you to go. And about that," she says, "your plan doesn't have anything to do with Herr Weber's pigeons, does it?" she asks, catching Peter off guard.

"It might. Or it might not," says Peter. "Why?"

"Well, I've been thinking lately about when I first met you and wondering why you were feeding Herr Weber's pigeons. I didn't understand why Otto wouldn't just do it himself, and then –"

"You know Otto?" Peter says.

"Of course I know Otto. Everyone knows everyone in my building. So why are you feeding his father's pigeons?"

Peter feels confused. "Wait, Otto lives in your building? And they're his father's pigeons? That can't be right. Are you sure? Otto told me he lives in Prenzlauer Berg with his family."

"What? No he doesn't!" Elke snorts. "Otto lives with his father in my building. His mother died when he was a baby."

Peter's mind is ticking over rapidly. "He told me that the old man who owned the pigeons was stuck in the West ... unless ... it's really his dad over there."

"I haven't seen him around," says Elke. "Otto must be beside himself if he's been separated from his father. They're best friends. They only have each other – oh, and the pigeons. But that still doesn't explain why Otto asked you to feed them. Or why he didn't tell you they belong to his father. Is there something you're doing for him in return?"

Then it dawns on Peter. It's as if he's just been startled out of a deep sleep. His heart is pounding against his chest.

"What? What's wrong?" Elke asks.

"Otto's making it for himself," Peter cries. "Not for me! I've got to stop him . . . NOW!"

Sie kommen!
THEY'RE COMING!

"Where are you two going?" Oma calls to Peter, as he and Elke rush out into the hallway. "What's the rush? Your friend just got here."

"I'm going to walk Elke back home, Oma," Peter shouts back over his shoulder.

"Thank you for the cake," Elke cries, charging down the steps after Peter.

When they bound out onto the street, Peter kicks into a sprint. Elke chases after him.

"Peter, wait up! What's going on?" she shouts, running as fast as she can.

The daylight is starting to fade as the sun begins to

set on a windy summer's day. They run together until Peter makes a sharp left into the street that leads to Otto's and Elke's building.

His mind is on Otto. How could he lie to me like that? he thinks, his shoes pounding hard on the pavement. He stole my idea!

They reach the building, and Peter charges up the stairwell. He bursts through the door onto the rooftop to see Otto standing there underneath a canopy of vibrant yellow, caught in the breeze.

The glider looks magnificent. Its bamboo frame is pointing in the direction of the border building. Otto appears to be using all the strength in his legs to stay in one place and is struggling to hold on to the crossbar below the frame. The strong breeze is making the fabric ripple. Otto's arms are looped in leather straps and he's poised as if he's ready to run and jump.

"No!" Peter shouts. "Stop! Don't!"

Otto is startled to see Peter. "Leave me alone, Peter," he orders.

"You can't do this to me," Peter cries, rushing over and standing in front of Otto. "You lied to me. You used me."

"I built it," Otto growls. "You could never have done this on your own. And you have your grandparents here. I have no one."

"But you said it was a stupid idea . . . that it wouldn't work. Please don't do this to me."

"It was a stupid idea, Peter. But I made it better. Feel that wind? It's so strong. It's the lift I need to make this jump. Now stand back!"

Peter tries to grab at Otto, but he pushes him away. Peter stumbles backward.

Otto takes a few steps back to take his run-up.

"Peter! Otto!" Elke cries, reaching the rooftop. "The Stasi! Mama says they're out on the street. They're searching the apartments. They're heading this way."

Peter is in such a panic, he can hardly think straight.

"Look after my pigeons, Peter," Otto pleads.

Peter glances up to see the pigeons circling above. They appear bewildered and disorientated, as if they can somehow sense the confusion playing out on the rooftop.

"Please, move out of my way," Otto begs.

"I'm not letting you jump," Peter cries, standing firmly in front of Otto and the glider.

"Let him go. We've got to leave," Elke pleads. "We'll be safe in my apartment, but they'll lock us all up if they find us here with him."

"Peter!" Otto shouts. "It's my only chance to get to my father."

Peter sees the despair in Otto's eyes.

No one understands that feeling better than Peter.

Elke races over to him and tries to drag him away by the arm. "*Wir müssen weg!* We have to get out of here," she cries.

Peter lets her pull him away, and together they run to the door and down the stairs. They can hear the police charging up from below. With only seconds to spare, just as the men storm past, Peter and Elke open the door and slip into the apartment.

Elke's mother hugs her tightly. She looks frightened and puts her finger to her lips to tell Peter to stay quiet. Peter can hear his heart pounding.

After the footsteps have passed. Peter pulls the door ajar, just a crack, and peeks out. He sees the last of the policemen disappear up the stairwell. He hears them shouting, and then . . . gunshots!

Peter gasps. "No! Otto!"

A minute later the police race back down the stairs again. But Otto isn't with them.

"They don't have him," Peter whispers to Elke, as her mother pulls him away from the door and locks it. "I hope he made it. I really hope it worked."

It's at least an hour before Elke's mother feels

it's safe for Peter to leave. When he steps out onto the street, he sees residents from other buildings clustered in small groups talking excitedly.

"What's going on?" Peter asks a boy about his age standing nearby.

"Someone escaped!" the boy says. "Carried away by a giant yellow wing – he flew right over the border building and into the West."

Peter's entire body jolts. Otto actually made it. We actually did it! he thinks. But just then something else catches his eye that makes him shudder.

"No!" he whispers.

Wolfgang and Ludwig are lying motionless on the ground.

Pfeil und Bogen
BOW AND ARROW

Later that night Peter sits at the kitchen table, picking at another slice of cake. He's in a daze and feels numb all over.

"Right. Opa is tucked in bed for the night," Oma says. "Now I think I might have some more of that Kalter Hund."

Oma grabs a fork, pulls up a chair and digs into Peter's slice. "So, are you going to tell me?" she says.

"Huh?" Peter says.

"Are you going to tell me why you're acting so strange? You rush out the door with that lovely Elke as if the building is on fire and when you come back you're all *bedrückt* – gloomy and blue. What's going on? Did she say something to hurt your feelings?"

"No, no. It's nothing like that," says Peter.

"Then what?" Oma presses. She leans forward and brushes Peter's hair out of his eyes. "What is it, *mein Schatz*?"

Peter has a strong urge to tell his oma everything, and tell her that he has no other ideas or plans. That he could never repeat what Otto did – Otto's right that he doesn't have the skills or the materials to build another glider. And even if he did, he couldn't, not now that the Stasi are on high alert. He's even more afraid that he will never see his mother and father and sister again. He can't stop thinking about Wolfgang and Ludwig's crumpled little bodies on the pavement and wondering where Felix is. He is desperate to tell Oma all of this, but he can't. He doesn't.

"Are you feeling sad that they're not here?" Oma says softly. "Is that it?"

Peter eyes begin to sting. He's fighting to hold back tears. I'm too old to cry, he tells himself. And maybe Max is right. Maybe I was only thinking about myself. We could all have been arrested and I could have been killed. Oma and Opa would have been left alone. I'm not a hero . . . I'm a rat. Maybe I deserve to feel like this.

"If I hadn't been so selfish that day," he says to Oma, "I'd be over there in the West with them."

"Oh my poor boy," Oma sighs, pulling Peter toward her. "I wish we were all there, safe and together."

—

Early the next morning Peter is shocked out of a deep sleep by knocking at the door.

Opa is still asleep and Oma must be down the hall in the bathroom. Peter walks through to the kitchen in his pajamas, his hair tussled, and opens the door. It's Elke.

"What are you doing here?" he asks.

"Where is it?" She looks panicked.

"Where's what?"

"My bow and arrow. It's gone. You're the only one who knew about it. So where is it? I need it back."

"I don't have it," says Peter.

"You must have it," Elke says, looking desperate. "You don't understand. I need that bow and arrow. My family needs it."

Something dawns on Peter. "Max!" he says. "He went back to the abandoned building after seeing me leave it."

"Who?" Elke says. "Who's Max?"

"Give me a minute to get changed and we'll go get your bow and arrow," Peter declares. "Well, we'll try to get them anyway."

—

Peter and Elke hide behind a large hedge across the street from Max's apartment building in the same neighborhood as Elke and Otto's.

"Are you certain that this Max friend of yours has my bow and arrow?" asks Elke.

"Yes, I'm certain of it," says Peter. "But he's no friend of mine anymore. He'd turn us in if he knew our plans, and he'd enjoy it."

"Do you know how lucky we are that they didn't find us on the rooftop?"

Peter sighs heavily. "Do you think Otto is with his father now?"

Elke nods and smiles. "I hope so."

"Yeah, me too. I wonder if he was injured when he landed. But why did they have to shoot the pigeons?"

Elke's mother had helped them to bury Wolfgang and Ludwig in the courtyard. But there was still no sign of Felix. Peter hopes he is alive, but tries not to think of him flying around, looking for food, confused and alone.

Elke starts to say something, but then Peter points across the road. "There's Max! Get down."

They watch Max hop on his bike and ride away.

"Right. Let's make this quick," Peter says. "I've been there before, so you distract his mother and get her to move away from the door, and I'll slip past and into Max's bedroom, find the bow and arrow, and get out of there. Got it?"

Elke nods, and the two of them cross the street.

"Yes, can I help you?" Max's mother asks Elke when she opens the door.

"Hello, I'm Max's friend Elke."

Max's mother looks happy that Max has a visitor. "Oh, hello, Elke. Max has never mentioned you before. Unfortunately, you've just missed him."

"I know," Elke says. "I just saw him. He borrowed a book of mine and said he left it on the kitchen table."

"Let me get it for you."

"*Danke*. I'll come with you." Elke follows Max's mother inside, but leaves the door ajar behind her.

As Elke and Max's mother walk to the kitchen, Peter makes his move. He races into the apartment and straight for Max's bedroom.

Ablenken
DISTRACTING

Peter's heart races as he rummages around the room. It's absolutely spotless. The bed looks as if it hasn't even been slept in. The walls are covered with posters of astronauts and a yellow Free German Youth flag and ten-year-anniversary poster – a teenage boy and girl looking proudly off into the distance with the Soviet and German flags flapping in the wind behind them.

Peter moves to check Max's wardrobe. When he opens it, a shoebox filled with die-cast toy airplanes topples over and hits the ground with a *bang*. Peter winces. He hopes Max's mother hasn't heard it.

He can hear Elke's voice, making small talk and doing her best to distract Max's mother long enough for Peter to search the room.

But the bow and arrow are not there. Peter claws through stacks of folded clothes to check the back of the wardrobe.

"Let's just check his bedroom," Peter hears Max's mother say.

"Oh, no, it's all right," Elke calls. "He can keep the book if he wants . . ."

The doorknob turns and Peter dives for the floor, rolling underneath the bed just as Max's mother and Elke step in.

"It could be in here," says Max's mother as she walks over to the bedside table. "Such a mess," she says, picking up a few of the toy airplanes.

Peter holds his breath as he watches their feet. Then he notices something. Lying there right under his nose is Elke's bow and arrow. He grins.

"Well, it doesn't look like it's in here," Max's mother says. "Are you sure he said he'd leave it for you?"

"Um, come to think of it, I'm not sure if he said pick it up today or tomorrow," Elke says, her voice cracking with nerves. "He was on his bike and riding so fast. Maybe I misunderstood him. Anyway, I better get going. I'll come back when he's here . . . if that's all right?"

"Of course, my dear. I must say it's nice to see that

my Max is starting to make friends with girls. Before I know it he'll be a man and starting a family of his own."

"Um, all right then," Elke says, obviously not sure how to respond to that.

Peter has to stop himself laughing. And I thought Opa was embarrassing! he thinks.

"Could I possibly have a glass of water before I leave?" Elke asks.

"Of course. Come with me."

As Elke and Max's mother make their way to the kitchen, Peter grabs the bow and arrow, crawls out from under the bed, sneaks into the hallway and bolts out of the apartment.

He waits for Elke behind the hedge across the road. A few minutes later she crosses the street.

"Did you find it?" she asks anxiously, stepping in behind the hedge.

Peter nods and points into the bushy branches of the hedge. "And I don't think anyone saw me hide it there."

"Yes!" Elke cries, hugging him. "What a relief!"

Peter smiles and once again feels his face flush bright red. It feels good to be hugged by Elke – but she quickly pulls away.

"Right," she says, already thinking of what has to

be done next. "We'll keep the bow and arrow hidden here, and I'll arrange for my uncle to come pick it up in his car. If I walk back with it I'll draw too much attention, and I'm sure the police now have my building under surveillance. So . . . I guess this is where we say goodbye."

"Goodbye?" Peter says. "What do you mean?" Then he realizes that she must mean that she's escaping soon. "As in goodbye-forever goodbye?" he asks.

Elke nods. Peter doesn't know what to say. All he knows is that he doesn't want her to leave.

"I'm guessing that this bow and arrow have something to do with your plan to get to the West, right? But I can't work out how," he says, trying to stall Elke for even a few more minutes. "How is an arrow going to help you escape?"

"Oh, Peter." Elke sighs. "I can't tell you that. I'm sorry. But . . . thank you."

She leans forward and kisses Peter on the cheek. "*Auf Wiedersehen*," she says.

———

Peter walks aimlessly around his neighborhood. He's feeling empty inside, as gloomy as the gray buildings that line the street. He tries to think of other ways to escape. But he's finding it difficult to concentrate – and no ideas come to him. He thinks of his parents and sister and wonders what they're doing now.

When Peter gets home, Oma is at the stove boiling potatoes. Opa is at the kitchen table reading the newspaper.

"There you are," Oma says. "You got up early this morning. Where did you go?"

"I went to see if I could find a job . . ." Peter lies, pulling up a chair and sitting down next to Opa.

Opa looks up at him and winks. He opens his hand to reveal the rubber spider.

Peter sighs. He isn't in the mood for jokes. He shakes his head.

There's a knock at the door. "Oh, Elke," says Oma. "Come in!"

"No, thank you. I can't stay. I just want to see Peter about something," she says.

Peter jumps up.

"Excuse us, Oma," he says, stepping out into the hallway with Elke and closing the door behind him.

"What are you doing here?" Peter whispers.

"Do you still want to get to the West? To be with your family?" Elke says.

"Of course I do," says Peter.

"Good, then come to this address tonight at

eleven thirty," she says, placing a small, folded piece of paper in Peter's hand. "Don't be late!"

Elke leaves and Peter can't believe his luck.

Flüchten
ESCAPING

Peter nervously looks at the cuckoo clock in the hallway. It's close to 10:30 p.m.

This is it, he thinks, tiptoeing past his grandparents' room.

He stops. His chest is tight. And his hands are trembling.

He wants to look in on Opa and Oma. This really might be the last time he'll see them. But Peter can't let this gut-wrenching thought delay him, not even for a moment. He can hear them snoring. He wants to go in and hug them and kiss them and say he's sorry for leaving. Perhaps I could leave a note? he thinks.

But he can't. It's too painful. If I do, I won't leave, he tells himself. So he takes a deep breath, and sneaks out into the still night.

Peter jogs most of the way to Bouchéstrasse, to the address Elke gave him. And along the way he feels as if he's in one of those dreams that could easily turn into a nightmare.

He ducks in between parked cars, slinks along walls, avoiding the streetlights, and dashes across the wide boulevards.

After almost an hour, he reaches his destination. The street runs parallel with a dark, unguarded section of the Wall – it's just across the street. He double-checks the address and walks into the building.

"Of course it has to be the top floor," he mutters as he climbs the stairs.

When Peter reaches the top of the stairwell he gently taps at the apartment door. It opens in a beat. It's Elke.

"You made it," she whispers. "Are you sure no one followed you?"

"I'm sure," Peter says.

"Quick. Come in."

Peter follows Elke into the living room and finds Elke's mother and a man standing there, looking out the open window.

"This is my Uncle Hans," says Elke. "This is his place."

"I hear we have you to thank," Hans says, turning to shake Peter's hand, "for retrieving these."

Elke's mother holds up Elke's bow and arrow. "And if we're ready, it's almost time," she says. "I'll grab the pulley and fishing line."

"Pulley and fishing line?" Peter says.

Elke gestures at the window.

Over the Wall, Peter can see apartment buildings in the West, about forty meters from their building.

"We're going to attach a cable and then slide along it, over the wall," Elke explains. "My father is in that building directly opposite. He's in the apartment two floors down from us. The angle is perfect. We need to be at a higher point so we can travel downward."

Peter looks nervously out the window at the long drop to the street. "It sounds dangerous."

Elke's mother steps in between them. "Probably. But we're doing it. And we're hoping not to get shot. Elke, get ready."

Elke turns to Peter. "Have a look in my backpack, over there on the armchair," she says.

Peter reaches for Elke's bag and is surprised when

he hears something moving inside.

He reaches in and feels the softness of feathers. He can't believe it! It's a pigeon, wrapped in a tea towel so it can't fly away.

It's Felix!

"What? How?" Peter says.

Elke shrugs. "He came back." She hands the arrow to her Uncle Hans, who begins tying fishing line to the end of it. "I couldn't leave him there. Now that Otto's gone and we're leaving, there's no one to look after him."

"Elke, enough chatting. We need you to focus now," Uncle Hans says gruffly. "Your father should be switching the light on at any moment. When he does he'll open the window and step aside. That'll be your cue to take your shot."

Elke winks at Peter. Peter smiles nervously. He's anxious for her, for all of them.

"There's the light," Elke's mother announces. "Elke, this is it. Take your time. I have faith in you."

Peter sees a man's silhouette in the window, then he's gone. Elke steps up to the open window with the bow in her hand. Uncle Hans gives her back the arrow, now with fishing line attached to it.

She points the bow toward the ground and attaches the back of the arrow to the center of the bowstring.

And just as Peter saw her do in the courtyard of the abandoned theater, she places the arrow on the string with three fingers, raises the bow and pulls back on the string.

She points the arrow at the open apartment window in the building on the West side.

Peter holds his breath and Elke releases her grip.

Familie
FAMILY

The arrow whooshes over the Wall and right through the open window. A perfect shot!

"YES! YES!" Uncle Hans says excitedly. "*Du hast es geschafft!* You did it! You did it!"

"Good girl," cries Elke's mother. "I'm so proud of you."

Peter exhales. Elke is incredible.

But Elke's mother says that the most dangerous part of the escape is coming up. In the other window the figure in silhouette moves around, and the fishing line tightens and goes loose as something is attached to the other end.

Minutes later Uncle Hans tugs on the line and

reels it back inside. Now joined to it is a thick cable.

Uncle Hans secures the cable onto an iron bar bolted to the living room wall. He picks up something that looks like a steel wheel with a rim, about the size of a small dinner plate.

"This is the pulley that will take us across – I made it," he says proudly, as he begins to rig it up to the cable. Attached to the pulley is a bar handle and harness straps.

"Will that be able to hold our weight?" Peter says nervously.

"It should," says Uncle Hans. He shrugs. "If it doesn't, we fall to our deaths."

"What are you worried about?" Elke teases. "You were going to fly over the border."

"All right, I'll go first," says Uncle Hans, tying the fishing line to the back of the harness and securing the straps under his arms. "If I can get across safely, then we know it will be secure for all of you. If not . . . well, remember me fondly. Here goes!"

Uncle Hans climbs onto the windowsill. It's a long drop down to the ground. He checks that there are no police or border guards on the street below. "I can't see anyone," he says.

He takes a deep breath and, tightening his grip on the handle, he drops out of the window.

Elke and her mother watch Hans travel down the cable. They gasp in unison as he whizzes over the Wall and, putting his feet up, vanishes through the window into the apartment building in the West.

"Wow! He did it! It works! It works!" cries Elke, hugging her mother.

Peter is in awe. His heart is racing. Soon it will be his turn and in no time at all he'll be reunited with his parents and sister.

"Okay, Elke, you're next," her mother says as she tugs at the line and reels the pulley and harness back to them with the fishing line.

Elke grabs her backpack – with Felix cooing inside.

"I'll see you over there," she smiles, slapping Peter's shoulder.

Elke's mother fits the harness straps. Elke steps up to the windowsill and her mother kisses her.

"*Eins, zwei . . .*" Elke begins to count quietly, her voice trembling.

"It's all right, my love," says her mother. "Deep breath. *Du schaffst es.* You can do this."

"*Drei!*" Elke whispers. And she jumps.

Peter and Elke's mother watch Elke soar across the border, flying like an angel, her red hair flying wildly behind her.

"Yes! She made it!" Peter whispers.

Elke's mother starts reeling the pulley and harness back to them.

"You must be so excited to see your family again," she says, as she tugs at the line. "They're lucky they're all over there together, supporting each other. My husband has been on his own. But we'll be all together again soon. Yes, a new life, a new start. Right, here we go."

Elke's mother bends to lift the harness inside. "It's your turn, Peter. Put the straps on."

But Peter's thoughts are back with his grandparents. He remembers with a wince Elke's words from the other night. He's picturing them asleep back home – cuddled into each other. Picturing them waking up and discovering he has gone. Not knowing where he is. He thinks of his parents and what Elke's mother just said – that they're lucky to have one another, to support each other. But who will support Opa and Oma when he's not around? He thinks about Hubert, dealing with his brother's death. Doing everything on his own without his best friend.

"Peter?" Elke's mother says. "Is everything all right?"

Peter looks up at Elke's mother, his vision blurred by tears.

"I . . . I can't go," he cries. "I have to stay. For Oma. For Opa. And for Hubert."

Tears race down Peter's cheeks.

"Please, find my parents and tell them I love them," he says. "And hug my sister for me. My father works as a concierge at a cinema on the Ku'damm. Tell them I miss them, and that they have nothing to worry about because I will take good care of Oma and Opa. Could you please tell them that?"

Peter wipes away the tears with the back of his hand. Elke's mother hugs him.

"And tell Elke . . . tell her that I'll miss her. And I'll never forget her."

"I will, dear boy," she says. "I will."

Hoffnung
HOPE

A week later Peter is pulling Hubert's recycling cart along the street where Otto and Elke used to live. Hubert is walking beside him. He looks up at the building that used to mean so much to him, but now he doesn't have any reason to go there.

"With all these bottles we've collected, I think we have around eight marks worth," Hubert says.

"I think more like ten marks, if you include all the scrap metal we found at the abandoned theater," Peter adds. "If we keep going this way, we . . ."

Something catches Peter's eye. A bird is circling above. It's flying in a certain, familiar pattern.

"What? What are you looking at?" asks Hubert,

following Peter's gaze. "It's just a pigeon. Why are you interested in a pigeon?"

The bird flies toward them.

"Quick!" Peter cries, pulling on the recycling cart.

When Peter reaches Elke and Otto's building, he stops to catch his breath before entering.

"What are you doing?" Hubert asks, as Peter leaves the cart by the door.

"I'm not sure," Peter says. He steps inside the foyer and makes his way up the stairs to the rooftop.

He bursts through the door and onto the roof, and there he is – a little gray pigeon, toddling about on the coop.

"Felix?" Peter whispers, moving toward him. "It is really you?"

He puts his hand out, and Felix flies up to land on his wrist. Peter strokes his soft feathers and Felix turns his head to look up at him, making quiet cooing noises. Peter wishes he had some seed to give him.

Then Peter notices something attached to Felix's leg. It's a small folded piece of paper secured by a band. Peter gently picks Felix up, unties the strap from his leg, places him in the coop and unfolds the paper.

It's a letter, written in tiny script.

Dear Peter,

I'm not sure if you will ever read this but, if you do, know my heart aches for you, my beautiful boy. Your father, sister and I miss you more than words could ever express. We met your friend Elke and her parents, and when they told us about your decision to stay with Oma and Opa, I cried and cried. But I am also so proud of you.

This Wall will not be here forever. And true love, the love of a family, can never really be divided. When that day comes, when the barrier between us falls, I will get to hug you again.

Be strong, my dear heart. Kiss Oma and Opa for me, for us all. Tell them that we love them and miss them every minute of the day.

All my love,
Mutti

Peter flips the letter over. On the reverse side of the paper there's a small illustration drawn by his little sister. It's his mother, his father, Margrit, Opa, Oma and him, all stick figures, smiling and holding hands.

Tears stream down Peter's face.

"Hey! What are you doing?" Hubert calls, stepping

out onto the rooftop. "We can't leave our cart down there in the street."

Peter quickly wipes his eyes, shoves the note in his pocket and turns to his friend.

"Come and meet Felix," he says. "I used to help look after him. Then he went to the West. Now he's back, but I'm not sure who will look after him now that his owner is gone."

"Why can't it be you? On the rooftop of your building?" asks Hubert.

"He's a homing pigeon," says Peter, wishing he really could take Felix home. "He'll just keep flying back here."

"I've read that some homing pigeons can be relocated – it's not easy, but they used to do it in the war all the time," Hubert says enthusiastically, leaning forward to pat Felix. "We could set up a coop and raise pigeons together. It could be like our own pigeon club. Of course, I'll name one after Ralf – he loved birds."

Peter smiles for the first time since Elke and her family left for the West. He knows there will be hard times ahead, but at least he and Hubert will have each other.

"Let's do it!" he says.

As Hubert makes his way down the stairs, Peter

picks up Felix and holds him gently in his hands. He looks back at the empty coop and the rooftop. He thinks of Otto and Elke, and his mother's words: *True love, the love of a family, can never really be divided.*

Peter cradles Felix close to his chest and walks after his friend.

FROM THE AUTHOR

Ideas strike you at the oddest times and places. Many of my stories have come to me while I've been traveling or on the move, when I can allow my mind to drift and let my imagination run. And my stories are so often born out of curiosity and asking questions.

A few years ago I visited Germany and went to Berlin. I did all the touristy tours and, like millions of visitors to that incredible city, I learned a bit about its fascinating history. I was particularly taken by the Berlin Wall and the idea that someone would cut a city down the middle and stop families from seeing each other, stop people going to work, or to visit their friends. I asked my local friends a lot of questions. Why did the government do that? How did they do that? And then I asked myself: What if this were to happen today? How would I react? What would I do?

I wondered what I would be willing to sacrifice to see my family again. Or to be with my friends. Would I risk living in a refugee camp? Would I live in poverty? Would I leave the people I cared about who wanted to stay? Would I even risk or sacrifice my life like so many East Germans did to get to the West?

One thing I knew – I would do anything to be with my family.

After the wall went up, East Germany became an increasingly dangerous place to be. The terrifying Stasi, the secret police, helped by people like Max who turned on their friends, made East Germany a very scary place to live.

There have been lots of movies and books about the Wall and the Cold War between the Soviets and America and its allies. I had a moment of doubt – thinking perhaps it wasn't my place, especially as an Australian, to write a story centered around this famous episode in European history.

Even though the East German refugees' dangerous quest for freedom and escape appealed to my sense of adventure, I put the story aside for a while.

Then one day I was talking to my neighbor in my building. He's a German Australian in his seventies who loves to walk his Labrador. One day we were talking about books, and I said I was thinking of writing a story set in Berlin. "Oh, Berlin," he said. "I'm from Berlin. Did you know I was a guard on the Wall?"

I couldn't believe it! What are the chances? I took this as a sign that I should start writing this story. I threw myself into researching more about the escapes and watching videos of people who shared their harrowing experiences. And, of course, along the way I was able to knock on my neighbor's door to ask him questions.

The escapes mentioned in this story are based on real-life events (successful and unsuccessful). I have taken liberties with the timeline and the details – not all of them occurred within the two weeks covered in Peter's story. I hope you will be curious to do your own research on the actual people who risked their lives to be safe or to be with their loved ones, and learn more about refugees everywhere who take those risks today.

The saddest thing for me about Peter's story is that I knew when I was writing it that it would take twenty-eight years before he would be able to cross the border again.

Like millions watching around the world, I saw the Wall come down live on television in 1989. I clearly remember the elation and tears of families and friends being reunited after so many years apart.

I like to think that Peter was among them, rushing to embrace his family. Perhaps he would have children of his own, who would be meeting Margrit's kids for the first time. I imagine Sabine, Elke and Otto there too. Or perhaps one of them had migrated to a country like Australia to start a new life like my neighbor did. I would love to know their stories! Maybe you can write them.

I hope that you will come away from this book with hope in your heart, knowing that goodwill and kindness will eventually find a way to break through any barriers that divide us. We all want a life in which we can be free to grow, play, laugh and love.

And, by the way, my German neighbor's name is

Peter and his Labrador is Otto. Thanks, Peter. They sounded like pretty good names to me!

Felice

Alles Gute! (All the best!)

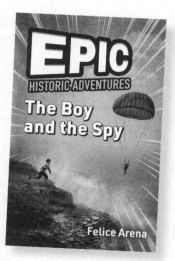

Life has never been easy for Antonio, but since
the war began there are German soldiers on
every corner, fearsome gangsters and the fascist
police everywhere, and no one ever has enough
to eat. But when Antonio decides to trust a man
who has literally fallen from the sky, he leaps
into an adventure that will change his life and
maybe even the future of Sicily . . .

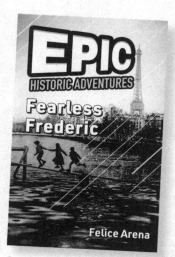

When the river rises and the city of Paris begins
to disappear under water, Frederic decides to
help those who can't help themselves. But as his
heroic acts escalate, so does the danger. Frederic
will have to battle an escaped zoo animal and
fight off pickpockets and looters but, as the
waters subside, can he find justice for his father
and find out what courage really means?